ACKNOWLEDGMENTS

I wish to acknowledge with deepest thanks various folks who unselfishly gave their time and expertise in editing and proofing this book. First, I would like to thank my wife, Leigh, who provided support and encouragement in addition to her editing skills. I also want to thank my daughter Patience Smith for her contribution of ideas to the original draft. And special thanks to Sarah Parsons West and Peter Smith without whose assistance this book would never have been finished. I am truly grateful to all of you.

Contents

CHAPTER ONE

A Time to Remember

The watery mist covering my eyes blurred my vision as I blinked repeatedly to clear them. I could hardly make out whatever was in front of me, yet I could see a slight shadowy movement in the room. My mind was struggling to clear itself. As my eyes worked to focus, I began to have brief moments of clear vision. I was in a room with machines all around. A woman dressed in white was reading something on a clipboard staring occasionally at the monitors. On the wall in front of me I could see a brown framed picture of a field of daisies and a blue sky. It was the sort of thing you might buy at a local department store. I could hear a constant beeping sound. Shifting my head to the right I saw a tube coming out of a machine leading to my right arm. A plastic bag full of clear liquid was slowly dripping down the tube through a needle and into my arm. I had been around long enough to know I was attached to an IV. It didn't take me long to realize I was in a hospital. "But why? How did I get here?" Numerous questions raced through my mind. I was struggling to remember.

With so little energy, I could hardly move. No one seemed to pay any attention to me. The woman in white didn't look at my face. It was as if I was invisible. I must have drifted off to sleep because last thing I remember was looking at a clock on the wall above a door. "7:34 a.m." in the morning. When I opened my eyes again it read "1:30" in the afternoon. After a few moments my eyesight once again became clear. Looking around the room I began to focus my thoughts. It was becoming easier. This time several people were coming in and out of the room and still no one seemed to notice I was awake.

I decided to try and sit up, which ended up being a foolish move. Immediately, I became dizzy and felt myself starting to tumble to the floor. I attempted to grab on to the small bed stand to steady myself. Were it not for a nurse who happened to notice my movement at that moment, I would have hit the floor hard. As she caught my arm and shoulder, she steadied me and helped me back into the bed.

Before she caught me, I felt a great pain in my lower section. It was then I realized I was attached to a catheter. "Why a catheter?" I thought to myself? In my attempt to get out of bed, I tore a needle from my arm and blood began dripping down. The nurse quickly applied a bandage.

I still couldn't remember much and had no idea why I was here! My mind was muddled again and I was beginning to get anxious struggling to make sense of it all. My heart was beginning to beat faster and faster.

It was then I heard the nurse almost in a panic yell, "Oh my God! He's awake!" Quickly people came out of nowhere into the room and began to stare at me. No one was saying anything -- just staring.

A fairly older man, perhaps in his early sixties and wearing a white coat, walked hurriedly into the room. He had a strange look on his face as he stared at me. With my head back on the pillow all I could do was stare back. "Please, clear the room," he said in a soft, gentle tone after quickly sizing up the situation. Everyone left except for this man who I assumed was a doctor by the way he was dressed, and the nurse who had helped me back onto the bed. I was still bewildered and couldn't talk. There were a few seconds of silence, which were broken when I heard him say with a huge smile, "Well, good afternoon, soldier. Did you have a good nap? I'm Dr. Goodson. You've been in my care since you arrived here."

All I could do was continue to stare at him for what seemed like an eternity. My eyes drifted between him and the nurse standing to his left. She wore a smile as well. But my mind was going crazy. "Hospital, IV, white coat, nurses, catheter, stunned gawkers!" I closed my eyes and tried to think. He could see the state I was in and simply waited for me to open my eyes again. He instinctively knew I had to have time to get my head straight. "I'll come back in an hour or two and then we'll have a talk. You've been through quite an ordeal, my young friend. We were beginning to wonder if you were ever going to wake up. But we'll get to that later," he said as he turned to leave the room.

"Doctor, where am I? How long have I been here?" I quickly asked.

He turned back towards me, "You're at a VA Hospital in Northbrook, Massachusetts. You've been in a coma for quite a few weeks. You were sent here from Walter Reed Army Medical Center. The right side of your head was severely damaged in an explosion. From what I understand, you were in a helicopter when it was hit. You and the pilot went down. As I was told when you arrived here only you survived…barely. Son, we'll talk some more after the nurses clean you up a bit. Try and relax. In the meantime I want you to try and remember as far back as you can."

As he left the room I asked the nurse if I could have a mirror. She pulled one from the small table beside my bed and handed it to me. Much of my head was wrapped in white gauze bandages with the exception of the top, with only a bit of red hair showing. I quickly put the mirror down.

A few moments later, a hospital worker brought a tray of food. I couldn't remember the last time I had eaten, yet I didn't feel hungry at all. I wasn't going to eat and was asking the delivery lady to take the tray back when suddenly a different nurse came into the room. She had apparently heard my conversation. "Sorry, soldier, but you have to begin eating. Doctor's orders. It's a special diet to get you back on track slowly. After all, it's been a long time since you had any real food. So, eat up." she said with the voice of authority. I could sense she wasn't one to be taken lightly, so I began to eat the meal consisting of very bland chicken soup, a few crackers, and strawberry jello. When I asked for a cup of coffee, she said that would have to wait until tomorrow. "The acid in the coffee might cause your stomach to react and make you sick." I would have given anything for a cup of hot coffee but decided not to push the issue.

It was probably good that she made me eat the meal. After a while I became less confused and was able to begin focusing my thoughts. I had so many questions to ask the doctor when he returned. Closing my eyes, I tried to think back as far as I could remember.

CHAPTER TWO

A Time of Innocence – 1965

*I*t was a hot day in mid-July of 1965 in Weldon Mills, Massachusetts. The heat this particular summer was almost unbearable. It had been one of the hottest summers anyone could remember. Like most teenagers, Tom and I were bored. School was out for the summer. I was entering my senior year of high school in a few weeks and Tom was going into his junior year. Neither of us had a steady job. We weren't really interested in trying to find one. We'd worked in the local tobacco fields the previous two summers, and it had not been a great experience. For eight hours a day, you dragged your butt along the ground moving from one tobacco plant to another picking out the 'suckers' that grew between the leaves and stalks. The rows were long and the sun burned your skin. These little invaders stunted the growth of the plant and needed to be pulled out or they would destroy the entire plant. By the end of the day, your hands were sore and you fingers were raw and stained green - - never mind how your butt felt. But this summer we managed to scrape up a few bucks mowing lawns and doing yard work here and there to get us through. Being semi-broke was much better than going back into the tobacco fields. We wanted to make the most of the summer. As for me, I didn't know what might lie ahead after graduation.

Tom Davis and I had been friends for about four years and were constant companions. Every afternoon when school let out we would head to the Foxrun Coffee Shop and hang out. Hijacking a booth, we would sip Cokes and watch the girls come and go. I'm sure we aggravated Mr. Sampson, the owner of the shop. We tended to commandeer one of three booths for long periods of time. We'd always try for the booth nearest the jukebox. But he was kind and never said anything to us. He had teenage daughters, so I think he understood. The coffee shop was a magnet for females. Tom and I took advantage of that. We both had an idea the summer of '65 could be our last one together. The hippie movement, the political upheaval, and Vietnam were all down the road. I was of draft age but Tom was classified as not eligible. He never really shared with me why he wouldn't be drafted and I didn't ask. I always suspected it was because of a medical condition. For the moment, however, our world was one of fun and innocence.

One particular day we needed a plan, so we once again headed to the coffee shop in Weldon Mills. It was a quaint, quiet blue-collar town, with a single movie theater that only opened on weekends; two drug stores, two small food markets next to one another, two banks, and a restaurant run by a Greek family who made spaghetti sauce that was out of this world. It was a town where no one complained of the music being too loud when the corner drug store played Christmas carols on an outdoor speaker, and no one felt accosted by teenagers hanging around on Main Street. Every year on July 4th, the town would close a section of Main Street from eight to midnight in order to hold a block dance. It was an event everyone looked forward to. People from neighboring towns would come for the evening as well. Many of the stores would remain open long past their normal closing times. Food booths selling hot dogs and hamburgers would line the street. Craft booths could be found with locals selling their wares. It was a fun time in a small town. When I was around ten or eleven, I would peer out my bedroom window from the apartment block where we lived listening to the music and watching folks dance into the night. There were no particular themes to the dances. The local band played square dance music, country, waltzes, polka and even some rock-n-roll. It was a happy town and small enough where we could call everyone our neighbor.

The town drew many tourists in the summer for two reasons, the first of which was an old trolley-car bridge that had been turned into a huge flower garden. Trolleys had stopped running years before, and the bridge remained unused for a considerable time. The bridge spanned the Deer Run River and connected Weldon Mills to the much smaller town of Ashland. It was decided flowers would be planted on each side of the bridge with a walking path down the middle where the trolley track once was. The bridge soon became a 'must-see' attraction and eventually began to draw folks from all over the world. It became a photographer's paradise. That was and is Weldon Mills' main claim to fame.

The other attraction was a geological wonder called 'potholes' that had evolved over hundreds of years at the south end of the river, just past the dam. The potholes were worn into the rocks by loose stones whirling in strong, turbulent rapids, streams or waterfalls. To us they were just something that was always there. The local residents paid little attention to them, but to geologists and others, they were a strong attraction to our little town.

While sitting in the booth sipping sodas and listening to "Unchained Melody" by the Righteous Brothers, as it blared from the jukebox, Tom and I decided that, as it was a really hot day, we would don our bathing suits and go swimming. Past experience told us the local swimming pool would be far too crowded, so we decided we'd head out of town in his father's '51 Chevy and drive to the nearby Brandon State Park. It had a decent man-made swimming hole and was only about 12 miles from town. We figured we had enough gas to get there and back. The price of a gallon of gas was around thirty-one cents, so we were good for a couple of gallons. All Tom and I could think about was jumping into the cool water and maybe, just maybe, there would be some girls there.

The subject of 'girls' was not a topic I was really comfortable with. Being a jock was not one of my assets. I did not possess the kind of physique or looks that would cause girls to take a second glance. I had muscles that resembled something the size of gumballs. In my freshman year, I had tried out for the football team. It was a good way to try and impress the girls. Big mistake! After being used as a human tackling dummy by several two hundred and fifty pound apes all wanting to become linebackers for the New York Giants, I decided to take up baseball instead. I may not have attracted the opposite sex, but at least my 149-pound body remained in one piece.

Maybe I couldn't attract the girls on my own, but I did have an ace in the hole that summer. Tom was a decent looking guy with black, wavy hair and a trim, muscular build, along with a decent smile and not a zit to be found. He always seemed to attract the young ladies. It was amazing how all he had to do was smile, and they flocked to him like hummingbirds to sugar water. Tom's smile made a huge impact. When he did smile all you could see was a perfect set of teeth whiter than snow. He knew the effect he had on the females, and took great advantage of that. This summer he seemed to be at his best, so I decided to make sure I was with him when he was in their midst. Certainly, he could spare one. Ever hopeful me!

We finished our sodas, stopped off at the local gas station to buy gas and headed up the trail to the park. We opened the windows all the way. Air conditioning was something only rich folks had. We cranked up the radio as loud as we could. As we sang along to "Girl Happy" we were full of excitement at the prospects of a hot day, a cool swimming hole, and maybe girls in bikinis.

"Slow down!" I yelled as Tom went screaming up the highway. He was as anxious as I was to get there. "We want to get there before all the babes are taken!" Tom shouted over the music. "Won't do us any good if we get stopped by the police! Besides, we need to conserve gas." I said.

We passed through the small town of Charlesville. The town was named after someone long ago, but no one seemed to remember who. Charlesville was the site of an Indian raid back in the early 1700s. Local lore has it that one of the town leaders, Jeremiah Penn, was scalped and died at the base of a tree. The trunk of that tree still exists. The town had a population of around 3,600 people. There was no bank, only a single food market, a gas station, post office, and a small cafe. At one time, it boasted one of the finest Inns in New England. Local history has it that many famous people would frequent the Inn on the way to Albany. It was rumored that the actor Clark Gable once stayed at the Inn while passing through the area. But lately the inn was in quite a state of disrepair, and no one but area folks stopped by for a drink or a meal. Charlesville High School boasted a student population of around 152. All in all, it was a nice, small town.

The Charlesville Police Department consisted of one full-time officer who used his own car equipped with blue lights that were strapped to the roof. If he carried a gun, I never saw it. He was a fairly tall man with a receding hairline and black-rimmed glasses. His uniform consisted of well-worn jeans and a red and white checkered hunting shirt with a badge pinned to the left pocket. When he talked, his words were always accompanied with a large supply of spittle. The one thing Chief Malcolm Sanders was very good at was issuing speeding tickets. In this he was merciless. He may not have been the greatest crime fighter, but he did bring a lot of income to the state, some of which came back to the town coffers. The town leaders seemed to be quite satisfied with that.

The major highway to the state park ran straight through the main street of Charlesville and if you weren't careful you could easily fail to see the 25 mph sign half-hidden by an overhanging tree branch as you entered the town from the east. Many outsiders also felt the sting of Chief Sanders' pen. We always suspected the town selectmen were in no hurry to remove the branch.

Tom slowed down and we smoothly sailed past the chief waiting in ambush in his car partially hidden by a crop of overgrown bushes. The front end stuck out and we could read --LICE. Smiling as we went by his cruiser, we let out a great "YEAH!" and kept going. Chief Sanders did not appear to be smiling. His real specialty was catching speeding teenagers. Not this time.

The remainder of the trip was uneventful, with the exception of a squirrel that almost gave up the ghost. I often wonder what goes through the mind of a squirrel when it stops in the middle of a road. Do these pesky little animals have the ability to make quick decisions? "Do I cross the road or do I go back?" This little guy made the right decision and took off back the way he had come.

"Slow down or we'll miss the main gate!" I yelled as we came up to the park.

"We can't go through the main entrance, Mike, we don't have the money to get in that way. I'm gonna park up the road and we'll walk in." We found a place to ditch the car on a small turnoff about a quarter of a mile from the gate. With nothing but our swimsuits on, and towels slung around our necks, we hoofed it back to the park. The temperature continued to climb, and we were dripping wet from our walk, but excited at the prospects that may lie ahead.

There were campers sitting around campfires. Some were cooking hot dogs on a stick while others were simply staring at the flames. "What is so fascinating about flames that we have to gaze at them as if we were in some sort of a trance?" I wondered, as I passed by. A few families appeared to be unpacking their tents and setting up for the weekend. As we walked along the dirt path toward the pool, we could hear children laughing and splashing around. Tom and I hoped it wasn't too crowded. We soon found some open grass and sat on our towels. We began to scan the pool area. "Hmmmm! No girls to be seen!" Tom muttered.

"Don't worry, I said, they'll be here." It's only noon. Lets go up to the camp store and see what's happening." A friend of ours ran the store. Andy Pierson was a sophomore in college and earned money by operating the store during the summer. He sold everything from toilet paper to candy bars. Andy was also another one of those guys who could draw the females to him. He was good-looking with light blond hair and deep blue eyes. But what attracted the girls to him most was his guitar playing. He could have given Chuck Barry a run for his money. You could hear his guitar from quite a distance away, but nobody ever complained. Andy would pick up his guitar and we would sing whatever song Elvis had out at that time. He was good at picking, while I was lousy at singing, but we had fun.

"Hey, Andy, how's it going?" I said as we sauntered up to the counter. I never heard his answer. He could have screeched into a megaphone and I still wouldn't have heard him. From out of the corner of my left eye I saw a movement. Instinctively, I turned my head and there they were, two of the most beautiful girls I had ever seen. Tom said later my jaw dropped so low it almost touched my knees! I must be in the middle of a heat-induced hallucination. I thought to myself.

She and another girl had come around the corner of the camp store. I didn't think they had noticed us standing there because they immediately began talking with Andy. The girl I had noticed appeared to be interested in the various brands of suntan lotion on display. I could feel my heartbeat increasing by the second. At this point I didn't care about Tom or Andy! I didn't care about the heat! I didn't even care that I was standing there with a stupid blue-striped bathing suit I had inherited from my brother who was now in the Navy on some aircraft carrier in the Mediterranean, or that my knees looked like tree limbs - knots and all. A bomb could have exploded next to me and I wouldn't have noticed. My eyes focused on the shorter girl. Nothing in the world could have taken my eyes from her! She was about five-feet four, had blonde hair not quite shoulder length and parted on the left side. Her blue eyes and long eyelashes were simply beautiful. I couldn't help but also notice how shapely she was. She fit the two-piece black bathing suit perfectly. I had to force myself to look away before she caught me staring at her. But I kept stealing short glimpses as she continued to talk with Andy. I could feel my heart continuing to beat rapidly. My pulse was going absolutely crazy.

As they were talking to Andy, I tried to summon the courage to speak to her. I couldn't let this moment pass. I had to say something. As soon as there was a break in their conversation I got up the courage to at least say "Hello." Tom said it sounded like something between a hiccup and a squeaky mouse! When I managed to say it a second time, I think it sounded somewhat normal. At least I convinced myself that it did. What was I thinking? What did it matter anyway? She was too beautiful to take notice of a guy like me. I was nothing to look at, being five foot six with freckles and red hair and a skinny frame. If I were to wear a red-checkered shirt and a red bandana I would have looked like Howdy Doody. And there were plenty of folks who always reminded me of that! So why would I think this gorgeous girl would even take a second glance at me?

I was never a big believer in miracles, but one occurred on that hot July day. Just as I thought my "Hello" had fallen on deaf ears, it happened. The girl I had been sheepishly staring at turned to me and said, "Hi, there!" And she said it with a smile! I thought my heart was going to suddenly stop beating. It was the first time in my eighteen years on earth that a girl ever said "Hi" with a smile! It wasn't the token response I had become used to. I could tell in the way she said it. I just couldn't stop staring!

She was standing there probably wondering what I was going to say next. I had no idea. My tongue was so dry it felt as if it was covered with sand. I wondered if I was ever going to be able to swallow again. Turning to Tom, I lightly elbowed him in the ribs. Tom would know what I should say! But he blew me off. He had already begun a conversation with the other girl. I was on my own.

As I was again gathering the courage to say something, a second miracle happened! I heard, "I'm Kathleen Flynn and this is my friend Sharon Morrison." Her smile still seemed genuine and her voice was soft and sincere. I was in total meltdown. "I go by Kate." Wow! I couldn't blow this moment! "Mi…Mike Thompson." I blurted. When she held out her hand, I stared at it a second or two and then reached to shake it. Her hand was so soft and warm. I didn't want to let go! But then came my first blunder. "Are you camping here?" I asked. What was I thinking? Of course she is camping here, you idiot. Most people come to a campground to camp. She must have sensed my awkwardness as she simply smiled and said, "I'm with my parents. We got here yesterday from Concord just outside of Boston. Are you camping?"

"Tom and I are from Weldon Mills. You passed by there when you came to the park. We came up here to swim because the local pool was too crowded." I began to feel comfortable talking to her. Kate was so easy to talk with. There was something about her that quickly made me feel confident. I couldn't really explain it but there was something.

While Tom and Sharon were talking, Kate and I decided to walk down to the pool and bring the suntan lotion she had bought to her mother. After a short introduction to Kate's parents, we decided to take a walk down by the river that ran through the campground. Out of sheer nervousness I began tossing flat stones to see how far I could make them skip across the water. To my surprise Kate joined in. We talked about everything young people talk about. As the minutes went by we covered the entire gamut of school, classes, music, college, careers, etc. We had lots of laughs talking about the dumb things we did as kids. She cracked up when I told her about the time I had placed my glasses on the back bumper of a pickup truck when I was seven years old so I could play sandlot football with some kids in the neighborhood. Well, the truck that had not been used for days suddenly took off and so did my glasses. Afraid to tell my mother about the loss, I snuck an old pair I found in a bureau drawer and went off to school the next day thinking I would be fine. But the ruse was a failure because the glasses I took were an old pair my mother had used before she got new ones, and they were pink. And of course, I couldn't see clearly. My teacher was not fooled a bit. I was sent home and had to confess to my mother and father. The good news was that a neighbor who had seen us playing found the glasses. Apparently they had fallen off the end of the truck when it had driven away. He gave them to my mother. When I got home she was waiting for me to 'fess up. Yet, because the glasses were found, I got off with only a talking to.

The only time our conversation got somewhat serious was

when I mentioned recently registering for the draft and was told I was a prime candidate to be called up. Vietnam was becoming a serious issue in Washington. Troops were being trained in jungle warfare and sent over. I had not thought too much about it. To me it was just a small country that I could not even locate on a map. Kate expressed some concern. I could see it in her eyes and hear it in her voice although she did not dwell on it, and began talking about her family.

CHAPTER THREE

KATHLEEN "KATE" FLYNN

We Flynn's came from a very proud Irish family. My grandparents had come over from Ireland in the early part of the century, having passed through Ellis Island. They were from County Cork and had left Ireland because of the terrible economic conditions. After a few years of living in the Boston area, they moved to Concord where my father George was born and raised. We lived in an affluent section of Concord, although we were far from affluent ourselves. I never knew how we ended up in an upscale community. My father was a welder but also worked for a chemical company. My mother Colleen was a homemaker until I turned 16. She then went to work as a secretary. The house we lived in was an old farmhouse built sometime in the late 1800s.

I remember many nights in the cold winters of the Northeast when my father would have the fireplace roaring. The snow would be almost up to the windowsills and if you were outside, the cold air would freeze your face in two or three minutes. No matter how well-built the house was, you could still feel the cold seeping in through the door stoops and windows. Dad would pile on the wood in the fireplace to the point where the flames would shoot two or three feet up the chimney. Mom was sure he would burn the house down. Many an argument was heard in that old house on a cold wintry day. But in the end Dad would win out and Mom and I were always quite warm.

I met Mike when I was sixteen, July of 1965, while camping with my parents 75 miles away, in Western Massachusetts. Mom had decided it would be fun to gather the camping equipment and trek off to a camp for a week. This was not the first time they had camped, having done so before I was born, but it was the first time for me. I had mixed feelings about it. All I could think of were bears, poison ivy, public rest rooms and no showers. Anyway, Mom had set the agenda for that summer. Happy or not I had no choice. However, she did say that I could bring a friend along with us. So, I asked my best friend Sharon Morrison. We had been friends it seems forever. Sharon was five feet seven inches tall, and slightly plump but she had a smile that would knock guys for a loop. Once you saw her smile you forgot about her plumpness. Sharon had a happy, bubbly personality. She was comfortable with who she was, and it showed. With Sharon along on the summer camping trip, I remember thinking it might just be bearable after all.

We left home very early. Sharon had stayed overnight so we could get up early and get ready. We had talked well into the night. I don't remember that we slept much at all. In the car Sharon talked about the possibility of meeting some guys at the campground. I just smiled, not saying anything, remembering that my parents were in the front seat. Sharon was from a family of Protestant Congregationalists. Maybe they were allowed to talk about things like that. I instinctively knew what my mother was thinking as she glanced at me through the rearview mirror: "Good Irish-Catholic girls didn't talk about such things."

We finally arrived at the campground after a 90-minute trip. It was mostly uneventful except for my dad almost getting a speeding ticket while driving through a small town a few miles before the campground. Just as he saw the half-hidden branch covering 25 mph sign, he also glimpsed a car beside some bushes attempting to hide. He also noticed the word 'Police' printed in small letters on the front right fender. He stepped on the brake hard and went from 50 to 25 in about two seconds. I remember his saying, "They need to cut that tree branch down so you can see the sign!" He drove by the police car with a bit of a smile.

Sharon and I helped unpack the car and move things into the cabin. It was a real log cabin with a fairly large front porch. Inside, there was a twin bunk bed that could hold two people in the upper and lower bunks. Sharon and I were relegated to the top bunk. Along the wall were some large cabinets. A single light bulb fixture hung from the ceiling. There was a fireplace with a small wood-burning stove with a stack of wood beside it. We quickly helped to unpack food. My father said it was very important to pack the food in the outside bin carefully because there were bears in the woods that quite often would come into the camping area at night to investigate, especially if they smelled food. The bin was made of metal and had a lock. The thought of bears gave me chills.

Sharon and I cautiously began to look around outside. I was quite relieved to see that our cabin was just down from the showers and rest rooms. In the main area of the campground there was a building where someone was selling camp items. There was also a man-made swimming pool down from the store. A few kids were in the pool and lots of parents were sitting around in chaise lounges. Some folks seemed to be napping while others were reading books and newspapers. Others were simply watching their children swimming in the pool. We decided we would go swimming tomorrow, but today we were just going to read and get some sun.

Having slept late into the next morning, Sharon and I decided to go to the pool right after lunch. After donning our bathing suits, we grabbed our towels and headed down to the pool. Spreading the towels on the grass, we sat there for a few minutes looking at the people frolicking in the pool. The sun was high in the sky. It was another hot day.

Awhile later, Mom and Dad came down to the pool and were sitting in their chairs watching the swimmers. Mom remembered she had forgotten to bring some sun tan lotion and asked if I would mind going to the little store and pick up a tube. Sharon and I walked over to the store and began talking to the young good-looking guy behind the counter. Off to my right I caught a glimpse of a red-haired guy with glasses in a striped bathing suit and I think he was looking at me. I remember he had a strange look on his face. He wasn't particularly handsome but he was sort of innocently cute. He was thin and not very muscular like the fellow who was with him. His auburn red hair was neatly trimmed and parted on the left side. He had sideburns that went down to the bottom of his ears. I tried not to make it too obvious that I was looking at him. The other guy was fairly good looking and had a manlier build, but for some reason I could not get my thoughts off the skinny guy. As he was talking to the fellow behind the counter, I immediately sensed a gentleness about him. I don't remember ever feeling that about a guy before. It was strange. For a split second our eyes met. I smiled.

I could see his freckled face was turning red. I think he wanted to say hello and was trying to summon up the courage. Against all of my Catholic learning, I decided to take the bull by the horns and make the first gesture by saying 'Hello." My mother would have had a major trauma if she had been there. Girls just did not do that kind of thing, especially young ladies with a good Irish Catholic upbringing. But she was not with me and I was not going to let this moment pass. There was something about this guy that made my heart beat faster and faster.

If he were too shy to say "Hello" I would do it first. But as I was about to speak, I heard a faint "Hello." It was a weak and nervous sound. After I told him my name he said stutteringly, "Mi...Mike Thompson." After a couple of awkward moments we began to talk. A few minutes later we decided to take a walk around the park. We left Tom and Sharon on their own. That was the very beginning.

CHAPTER FOUR

SHEER JOY

I found Kate was unlike any other girl I had ever met. She was genuine and not silly like some of those I had grown up with. "I think she really likes me," I was telling myself.

After Kate introduced me and gave her mother the lotion, we sat by the pool and talked for a while. We decided to take a walk down to the river and listen to the rushing water. We tossed a few stones trying to skip them across the river. We talked about everything we could think of. I noticed her cringe when I mentioned I had registered for the draft. She knew what was happening in Vietnam. But it was a beautiful time and I never wanted it to end. Then I heard Tom yell "Mike, we gotta get back! My Dad will need the car to go to work. If I'm late he'll kill me." His Dad worked the evening shift at a local textile mill. Wow, it must have been around four o'clock. "Okay…. be there in a sec," I yelled.

I didn't want to leave Kate. "I guess I have to go. Darn time flies so fast! How long are you here for?" I quickly asked. "We're leaving Saturday afternoon. Mom and Dad want to go to Mass early Sunday morning back home," Kate said.

I asked her if she would mind if I came back the next day. "My Dad is off work and I think he'll let me use our old Rambler," I said as we walked back to the campsite. She said she thought that would work. "We are all going to town for breakfast and shopping in the morning, but we should be back by noon." I wanted to say something memorable to her, but all I could come up with was, "Great!" I can't even remember if I said good-bye. I am sure I must have. What I remember is walking away with my heart pounding and my pulse flying off the charts. The next day seemed like a million years away.

Tom and I didn't say more than ten words on the drive back to Weldon Mills. We were both somewhere in space. I was reliving every second that Kate and I had been together. I suspect Tom was thinking about Sharon, which is probably why we totally forgot about Chief Sanders. By the time we saw his police cruiser again with its front end barely visible from the side of a small tool shed, the chief had our speed locked into his radar gun. We saw the blue lights come on as soon as we passed him and knew what was coming next. Tom let out a "Damn!" and pulled over to the side of the road. "Forty-seven in a twenty-five mile an hour zone." the chief said. I saw a bit of a smile as he was filling out the ticket on the hood of Tom's car. I secretly hoped he burned himself on the hot metal. Tom drove the rest of the way in silence. "Heck of a way to start a romance, ain't it, Tom?" Tom didn't think that was funny. He must have been thinking about what he would tell his dad.

I realized we had never even got into the pool at the campground. But I didn't care, not a single bit! My heart was pounding and my insides were churning in joy.

At supper that night, my mother appeared somewhat bewildered. I heard her whisper to my father sarcastically "What's up with Mike? He's actually smiling." He just looked up at me and didn't answer. He had a long work night ahead and was only interested in eating dinner. A full stomach must have put him in a good mood because he said I could use the car tomorrow.

After the long, exciting day, I was tired and needed sleep. However, the excitement kept waking me up for most of the night with thoughts of Kate. Waking up around 11:30 and after showering and downing a bowl of cereal, I hopped into the car and left.

I drove being mindful of Chief Sanders and yesterday's encounter. All in all, it didn't matter because Super Cop was nowhere to be seen.

Everything in me wanted to put the gas pedal to the floor in order to get to the park faster. Common sense prevailed. Once again, I left the car on the side of the road beyond the park and quickly trotted to the pool area.

Kate and Sharon were wading in the pool. Sharon yelled to Kate, "Hey, Mike's here!" I am sure Kate saw the smile on my face as I slowly walked into the water. She was not wearing a bathing suit, but blue shorts and a white t-shirt.

"Hi there, Mike. You made it," Kate smiled. Little did she know that I would have walked the fifteen miles in tropical heat to see her. "Hi!" I said. Wanting to be polite, I went over and said "Good afternoon" to her mother and father sitting on lounge chairs a short distance away. I think they could sense I had a "crush" on their daughter. They were probably on their guard and were watching me closely. I figured the whole thing had been blown later when we were frolicking in the pool. Why guys thought it was cool to do cannonballs is beyond me. There was a tremendous splash and when I came up, Kate was standing there drenched. She had a somewhat bewildered look on her face. It was then we realized that she had not been wearing anything under her white T-shirt. When it got wet you could almost see through it. Actually, you could see through it. Turning away so as not to stare, I heard her Mom quietly say, "Kate, you might want to wrap your towel around your shoulders and go put your bathing suit on." When Kate left, I went over to apologize to her parents. The father glanced up at me with one eye raised. After a stare, her mother went back to reading her book. A few minutes later, Kate came back wearing her bathing suit. I told her how I was sorry for getting her all wet. She simply smiled and said, "It's okay. I needed to get my swimsuit on anyway."

Tom came up later that day after running some errands for his parents. I suspect he had not yet told his parents about the ticket. He and Sharon wanted to spend time in the pool. This was great because Kate and I wanted to be alone. We walked a few of the many trails in the park, always on the alert. During the walk she told me she was afraid there might be bears in the park area and she was afraid to walk too far from the main camp. I assured her that they would not come close during the day with all the people walking around. She seemed relieved to know that. I wasn't too sure that what I said was true, but it made Kate feel better. We talked on and on. I asked her if I could write to her during the school year and she said it would be nice. She gave me her address. I didn't have to write it down. That address was etched in my mind as sure as my own name. It would play an important role in my life, but of course, I didn't know that at the time.

I don't know how to explain it, but as those few hours went by we both could feel something develop between us. We were so much alike in many ways. We liked the same music, the same kind of books, TV shows, long walks, the pretty seasons of New England, and much more. Most of all, we enjoyed being with each other. Kate admitted that when we first met her heart began pounding very hard. She said she saw a gentleness and kindness in me. I had never thought of myself like that. Being both young and inexperienced we could not put a name to the feelings we were experiencing. We knew our feelings were not lying to us. Our hearts knew what was happening.

The afternoon sped by and soon it was time for me to bring the Rambler back to my dad. I had told him I would be back by 5:00 and it was already 4:15. We tried to say good-bye a hundred times, but always delayed. I couldn't leave without saying what I wanted to say. She needed to know what I felt in my heart. Somehow I had to come up with the courage to tell her. I took a daring step and reached for her left hand. I stared into her eyes and with a lumpy feeling in my throat I managed, "Kate, this may sound silly, but I care for you very much. I know we have only just met and I can't really understand it, but I know that my heart pounds to pieces when I think of you. Darn, I wish I had better words!" I continued to stare at her. I put my arms around her shoulders and drew Kate a little closer to me. I know it was a bold step, but it was as if something had taken control of me. I held her gently. To my astonishment she slowly wrapped her arms around me, too. We stood there under a huge maple tree holding on to one another. I was wishing the time would stand still forever. "What am I doing? This isn't me!" I thought. "Where is this boldness coming from?" As our lips lightly touched, I closed my eyes. I felt like our hearts were sealed together forever. I entered a world I had not known. It was my first real kiss. It was her first real kiss. I just knew this beautiful, precious moment came once in a lifetime. I knew this was our moment and our time.

Driving home slowly, I was savoring the last two days. I relived our brief time together over and over again. So much had happened. Strangely, as I was driving, a familiar song began to play on the radio. "Sealed with a Kiss" was about two people in love and having to say good-bye for the summer. It was a sad song. I wanted to turn the radio off, but I was mesmerized by it. Little did I know that it would be quite a while before we would see each other again.

CHAPTER FIVE

KATE'S AMAZEMENT

"*I* can't believe I kissed Mike on the lips." as we'd only met the day before, but something happened between us that brought down all my defenses. There was something that drew me to him in an instant. I cannot put the feelings and attraction into words. "Was it just a simple momentary summer romance? Were my hormones coming to life?" I asked myself. These were feelings I had never experienced before. They were new and exciting.

There were guys in school I occasionally dated, but there were never any feelings beyond the schoolgirl kind of thing. Holding hands or a kiss on the cheek here and there perhaps, but never on the lips. I never got touchy-feely on those dates. I suppose I did what was expected of a girl on a date back then. A couple of guys tried to go beyond that, but I was smart enough to hold them off. I was a young girl whose parents took great measures to prepare me for what guys might try to do. I took what they had taught me to heart. Although I felt they were old-fashioned and out-of-touch with the changes in modern day relationships, I listened. It was inbred in me that good Catholic girls did not do serious petting or have pre-marital sex, and that it was sinful to do so.

I remember how hard it was for us to part. All the time we were trying to say goodbye, I was wondering if I would ever see him again. I know there must have been a reason for our meeting. There just had to be. One thing I knew was that the heart didn't deceive. I remember thinking there were so many things to keep us apart. There was the distance of 75-85 miles between our homes. The Draft was in full swing and Mike was the right age to be drafted soon after high school graduation. And there was the possibility of his being sent to Vietnam.

We shared letters over the rest of the summer. He wrote that he was most definitely going to be drafted unless he got some sort of a deferment, but that was out of the question. Mike said the local draft board had already sent out notices of that possibility. He was not alone. Three others in his high school class had received those notices as well. Mike decided that he would enlist in the Army rather than allow someone else to decide which branch of service he would be drafted into. We promised we would never lose contact with each other in the days that would follow. I became anxious for him and for us.

CHAPTER SIX

A JOURNEY INTO HELL – 1966

$\mathcal{S}$leeping lightly, I suddenly became aware of the landing gear being locked into place. Seated just above the plane's wheel well, I could hear the whining of the gear's motor. We had left Maguire Air Force Base outside of Fort Dix, New Jersey, in the early morning seventeen hours earlier. After stops in Anchorage, Alaska and Tokyo, Japan we finally touched down at Tan Son Nhut Air Base just outside of Saigon, South Vietnam.

It was a heck of a way to celebrate Thanksgiving Day. I was not going to be with my family or home for my mother's wonderful turkey dinner. Her Thanksgiving dinners were definitely everything to write home about. With four boys who had appetites big enough to feed the entire Dallas Cowboys football team, she somehow always managed to get a huge turkey and stuff it until it looked as if it would explode. Add all the other fixings to that along with her wonderful homemade apple and pumpkin pies, we ate like kings! I always looked forward to Thanksgiving at our house. I was going to miss that this year and also the next year, because my tour would end the day before Thanksgiving and hopefully I would be heading back to the world I recently left behind. But on this flight, dinner was simply something strangely brown that resembled a kind of meat, along with instant potato and orange jello. The vegetable was turnips. Why turnips of all things? I had always hated turnips. I hated them so much as a kid I would stuff them into my pants pockets when no one was looking and then pretend I had to go to the bathroom, where I would dump them down the toilet. My mother could never quite figure out why every so often my pockets seemed to have a yellowish color. I looked at those turnips just hoping this was not a harbinger of things to come and passed on the dinner that day. But more than anything, my mind was focused on Kate. I didn't know when or if I would ever see her again.

It had been a long summer after high school graduation. Here it was November. Only a few months earlier I was simply a nerdy, skinny, red-haired, freckled face kid finishing high school. I had graduated with a general diploma. My school counselor made it clear I was not college material and should think of working in one of the local factories or joining the military. My father and brothers had been working in a local factory most of their lives. It was an honest and good living, but I wanted more. President Lyndon B. Johnson had recently committed more troops to combat roles in Vietnam and most guys my age were getting called up. If you were drafted you took whatever job they gave you. I decided to check out my options if I were to enlist voluntarily. I had no idea what I would do as a soldier, but after many tests and evaluations oddly enough it was decided that I would make a good infantry soldier. So I enlisted for a three-year stint in the Army. After completing eight weeks of basic training at Fort Dix, I was sent to Fort Benning, Georgia for advanced infantry training. It was there my life took a whole new direction. Somehow I managed to excel in the physical part of the training. It seemed I had gone though a complete metamorphosis. I painfully developed muscles I never knew I had. The time spent in training and with the help of the drill sergeants, I had gained such confidence in myself I had never felt before. Push-ups, pull-ups, sit-ups, running miles and miles all slowly made changes in my body. You gain a boatload of confidence climbing up and down a 50-foot cargo net. Crawling through mud under barbed wire with live machinegun fire just above your head made you alert and cautious. We were not allowed to fail. We were broken physically only to be rebuilt stronger. My arms became stronger and my mind keener. During weapons training, I learned I had a real knack for shooting weapons, especially my M-14 rifle. Back home, shooting a rifle and hunting was something every boy did. We were all familiar with weapons, mostly rifles and shotguns. We began learning to shoot at an early age. I was about ten or eleven when I fired my first rifle. It was a .22 caliber Remington single-shot rifle. During advance infantry training, I was able to score Expert. I could toss a grenade far and fairly accurately. The training was tough. It tested your metal. You were taught that the enemy had one goal in mind and that was to kill you. Your weapon was the only thing between your life or your death. You must shoot first. This was what the infantry was all about. That was how you survived in combat. After two months of intense combat training, the Army felt we were ready to put it all to good use. Graduation was a proud moment for those of us who successfully met the many challenges. Attaching the blue infantry braided lanyard to our shoulder was the culmination of our efforts. We were young and eager and also very idealistic. And we were ignorant.

So now, here I was, waiting for the plane to finish taxiing. My half-opened eyes focused on the stewardess standing by the door waiting for the signal from the cockpit to open and let us off. "It'll be another fifteen minutes." the stewardess said. I suspect most of the guys were eyeing her beauty because they knew she might well be the last "round eye" they would see for a year or so. I couldn't help but think for some it might be the last time. Paying no attention to her, I kept thinking of what may lie ahead? Where would I spend the next 12 months in 'Nam?

Staring out the window, I could see black bags neatly lined up in a row. I slowly counted 15 and didn't have to ask what was in those bags. They were soldiers going home for the last time. It was a stark reminder that this was no game. These bags contained the remains of lifeless men who only a short time ago had left their loved ones; mothers, fathers, brothers, sisters, wives and girlfriends in the hope of seeing them when their tour was finished. For those fifteen men, it would not be the reunion they had hoped for; it would be taps and tears. After stepping out of the plane and onto the tarmac, how would my life change? Would there be a black body bag for me up ahead?

Still staring at the door waiting for the stewardess to open it, I began to think of Kate. We didn't see each other again after the previous summer encounter. Our letters to each other had been almost daily. We wrote about everything we could think of. Kate would share her day from the moment she woke up until she went to bed. Most all of her letters were written at night just before she went to sleep. Our love for one another grew through our letter writing.

My thoughts of Kate were suddenly interrupted by the stewardess's announcement that we could now collect our carry-on baggage and depart the plane. It was strange that her last comment on the intercom was simply "Good luck." If I were to survive this war, it wouldn't be because of luck. Shooting dice, drawing the winning cards in poker, winning a lottery -- that was luck. But in war it was all of your training. You survived only if you could shoot quicker and straighter than the enemy. For me, that was the sum total of what it meant to be a soldier in Vietnam. Luck had nothing to do with it.

As my turn came to leave the air-conditioned plane, the extreme heat and odor of the country caught me by surprise and for an instant took my breath away. It is impossible to adequately describe the odor I was smelling but every so often on a hot day even now, a certain smell will remind me of my first moments in Vietnam. Adding to that memory was an Army K-9 guard dog barking profusely and lunging at a poor unsuspecting elderly Vietnamese woman carrying bundles on her head. Whether the military policeman walking the dog was going to be able to control him was questionable, but in the end he did. I watched as the poor woman began shaking almost beyond control. She had such a terrified look on her face. She was so frightened and caught off guard that she could not even let out a scream. Military trained dogs could not tell the difference between North or South Vietnamese people. They could not tell the friendlies from the enemy.

We were herded onto a bus that had several armed guards loaded with ammo packs, flak vests, steel helmets, and each carrying a full metal jacket in their M-14. A full metal jacket was a magazine full of ammunition inserted into your rifle. All of the windows were covered with chicken fencing wire. I asked the driver about that and he said sometimes the VC would run alongside of the bus and toss a grenade through a window. "Damn!" I said to the guy sitting next to me. "This is getting serious! This ain't training anymore!" He slowly shook his head as he stared out the window.

We arrived at the 90th Replacement Battalion outside of Saigon a few minutes later. The 'Repo Depot' was between the town of Bien Hoa and the big U.S. base at Long Binh. Almost every soldier coming to or leaving Vietnam passed through this station. Here we would receive our next unit assignment telling us where we would spend the next 12 months. To our left as we entered the compound with all of our gear, we could see some very happy soldiers decked out in their khaki uniforms. Combat ribbons adorned their shirts. Duffle bags were stacked waiting to be put on the plane which would take them back to the "World." Their tour was over and they had survived. I only had three hundred and sixty-four days to go.

I was not to receive orders to my next assignment until the next day, so I found the tent I was temporarily assigned and laid down on a cot. We were all tired after the long flight. Sleep was all we could think of and yet few of us could actually do it. There were too many thoughts and questions going through our heads. Where would we be assigned? How would we get there? What was this about the short life expectancy of an infantry soldier? These were all questions that would be answered in a short while. However, for the moment all I could think about was Kate and what she was doing? Did she remember our kiss and words at the park last year? Did she miss me? Did she still have the same burning embers that I had? I tried to put her out of my mind, but I couldn't.

After finally drifting off to sleep, I awoke around 6:00 a.m. I had missed dinner the night before and was about to miss breakfast. I had not taken my khaki uniform off before falling asleep and this fact did not go unnoticed by the barracks sergeant. He was not a big man but his voice was loud and clear! "Private, where the hell do you think this is…the Hilton?" he bellowed. "Get your butt out of bed and get over to the chow hall! Get into the proper uniform, now!" "Yes, Sergeant!" I answered. I jumped out of bed changed into my jungle fatigues. Jungle fatigues were olive green with numerous pockets in the shirt as well as the pants. They were loose-fitting and light. They were supposed to camouflage you when you were in the jungle. I packed away my khaki uniforms knowing that I wouldn't wear them again until November of 1967. That seemed like a lifetime. I headed to the chow hall and true to Army tradition, there was a line of us new guys all waiting to get breakfast. I was hungry and waited in line with everyone else. At the serving tables, there were powdered eggs, greasy bacon, cold toast and something that resembled hash. After taking a bit of each, I filled a hard, plastic brown mug with coffee and loaded it with milk and sugar. The food wasn't too bad or maybe I was just hungry.

A bit later, I reported to the Replacement Battalion Assignments building where I sat and waited to receive my next duty assignment. Suddenly, a soldier yelled out, PFC Thompson, Michael!" "Here, Specialist!" I answered. "You are headed to the 1st Cavalry Division in An Khe. You leave this afternoon at 1600 hrs. Here are your orders. Be at the transportation point on time."

As it was only 9:30, I had lots of time to prepare for the trip. The first thing I needed to do was find out where An Khe was. I found a map in the recreation tent. An Khe was a town in the Gia Lai Province in the Central Highlands region. The 1st Cav got there in 1965 and established a base camp at the foot of Hon Kong Mountain. This mountain was important to the military, as it was an important radar sight.

Soldiers assigned to the 1st Cav did not usually remain in the base camp but spent most of the time out on missions or, as I soon learned, "in the boonies." Right then, I wished I had not been such a hot shot with weapons. Inside, I knew what might be up the road, but felt I was prepared. At least I told myself I was.

I was assigned as an infantryman to Alpha Company, 1st of the 7th Cav. The 7th Cav had a famous history. It was the 7th that rode onto the Little Big Horn in June of 1876 with Lieutenant Colonel George A. Custer. A large band of Indians overwhelmed Custer's forces and he and most of his unit were decimated. History shows Custer made some tactical errors, which proved costly. The Alpha Company I was now assigned to had been involved in a fierce fight fifteen months earlier known as the Battle of Ia Drang. In August of 1965, the battalion had come under heavy attack from a reinforced enemy infantry battalion of the North Vietnamese Army. The battle lasted for several hours. They would have been surrounded and overcome had it not been for massive artillery and air support. There were casualties and many wounded soldiers, but in the end it was a victory for the American troops.

I had expected there to be a transition time for us new guys. I had hoped to be able to settle in and get used to my new surroundings, but that was not the case. The platoon was short of men and even the new guys would be going on patrol. The rumor we would be going out on patrol early the next day turned out not to be a rumor at all. My platoon leader told us to pack light. We would be leaving at 5:30 in the morning. We were told to take three bandoleers of M14 ammo, two grenades and three cartons of C-rations. "Be sure to bring some extra pairs of socks, too," he yelled.

Being an experienced combat vet he knew what we had not yet learned. The jungle can be vicious on your feet. It rained almost daily and you had to march through water and mud. Trench foot was common if you didn't keep your feet dry. Having trench foot meant you became incapacitated and couldn't do your job. At that point, you were no longer an asset to the mission and someone else had to pick up your responsibilities. It could also lead to gangrene if not treated. You couldn't treat it properly in the jungle. I packed two extra pair.

The great thing about being in the "Air Cav" was that you did not get to the patrol area by walking. The 1st Calvary was Air Mobile. Air Mobile meant that we would be transported to the Landing Zone (LZ) by helicopter. "Hueys" to be exact. Their nomenclature was actually "HU-1." Hueys were mainly gunships that often carried 2.75-inch rockets and various caliber machine guns. They also were used to transport troops and carry the dead and wounded out of combat areas. After a quick breakfast and at the designated time, we set out. My first patrol had begun. If you had asked me if I was scared, I would have said no. I would have been lying.

CHAPTER SEVEN

THE ENCOUNTER

Six of us were piled into one of the choppers, gear and all. It was tight. I was seated on the right side facing out. The door was not closed and my feet could easily have dangled out. I strapped myself in as tight as I could. My helmet was pressing against the back wall. It was not at all comfortable, but it was better than hoofing it. That would come later.

"OK everyone, close your eyes!" the door gunner yelled. I thought that was a strange comment, but as soon as the rotors began moving the blades I understood. Sand and dirt blew everywhere. The engine was loud and the ship vibrated violently as it reached the point of lifting off ground. The whining sound began to hurt my ears. I could see the ground below moving farther and farther away as we lifted off and banked to the right. The only thing holding me in the side seat was a small safety belt. Were that to break, I would have one of the shortest tours on record. With the door being left open, I could still see ground, which was now above my head. I was glad when the ship came out of the bank. The pilot jokingly said, "Welcome aboard my ship. Sorry guys, but the stewardesses have the day off." I closed my eyes and heard myself say, "This is it! This is what war is all about. No more training. No more practice runs. This is it."

Thirty-three minutes later we touched down at Landing Zone Julie. We were told it was a hot LZ, which meant there was possibly enemy activity in the area. "OK, everybody off!" shouted the door gunner. "We gotta load some dead and wounded." I looked over to my left at the makeshift tarmac. I didn't like what I saw. Laid out in a row were three black bags all zipped up and tagged. They would accompany the wounded. This was getting too real.

I unbuckled the strap holding me in place and leaped out. While in mid-air, my left foot came in contact with the helicopter's skid and I went face down into the dirt. My rifle barrel hit my chin and I let out a loud "Damn!" I felt so stupid. I could hear a seasoned vet off to the side laughing! "Hey, new guy, get with the program! You gonna die for sure if you keep that crap up!" As much as I hated to hear it, I knew he was right. If that rifle had gone off my face would have been cauliflower and spaghetti sauce. Fortunately, I hadn't chambered a round. That would come back to bite me a little later.

In the midst of all of this, my thoughts again went to Kate. Where was she? What was she doing at this moment? Did she still think of me? I would write to her when I could.

But my thoughts about her were short-lived. "Okay, especially you new guys! Listen up!" the squad leader yelled. We would be "new guys" until they saw how we performed. Seasoned soldiers wouldn't trust a new guy until they saw how he reacted in a combat situation. Combat was a 'rite of passage.' "The VC are about two hundred clicks east of here. Intel says it's only a small patrol but they've been wreaking havoc in the local villages. We're going to help them see the error of their ways. You new guys, pair up with a vet! Follow their orders exactly and you might live through this. All right, let's go!"

We fanned out and began walking slowly until we came upon a rice paddy. Rice paddies are covered with water to support the rice plants. There were Vietnamese working nearby in the field. They didn't seem to be paying attention to us. I guess they had seen this many times before. As we walked closer to the end of the field and nearer the jungle, I noticed the seasoned vets were no longer talking. They were in a slight crouch and watching every step they took. "The VC have a habit of laying mines at the end of the rice fields. You get through the rice paddy thinking you are safe and all of a sudden "Ka-boom!" "Follow me and step where I step," the corporal said. That was one order I had no problem obeying. This was his second tour in 'Nam. He knew what he was doing and that gave me a lot of comfort. My t-shirt was soaked with sweat and making me so uncomfortable. It poured down my eyelids and burned. My eyes kept blinking to clear my vision. The more I wiped away, the worse it got. My armpits were full of sand from the chopper ride. I was getting nervous now. It was the first real fear I had since coming "in country." We were fortunate to get into the jungle unscathed.

We were about a half-mile into the thick jungle when the company commander signaled for us to stop where we were. Did he spot the VC, I wondered? Nope. We were told to remain in place. Even in combat we got a break! "So far so good," I said to the corporal sitting on the ground a few feet away. He looked at me quizzically and said, "He's not the brightest commander we've had. Did you notice that he didn't have First Sergeant Kerwoski set up a perimeter guard? It's a good thing that 'Top' is on the ball." 'Top' was an affectionate name for the First Sergeant of the company. "This was Sergeant Kerwoski's third and last tour. He would retire from the Army when we got back to base camp. We found out later on he didn't have to go on this patrol, but chose to because of us inexperienced new guys.

Thirty minutes later we were back on patrol. We continued to be spread out as we quietly and cautiously made our way forward. The jungle was thick. You couldn't see more than a couple of yards. Trying to move without making a lot of noise was difficult when using machetes to cut through the thick jungle brush. We were told to keep each other in sight, however, as there would be less chance of shooting one of our own. It is funny how certain thoughts came to you out of the blue. As I was making my way through the brush, I suddenly realized how easy it would be for a branch to dislodge the safety pin ring on one of the two hand grenades I had attached to my web belt. The pin would release the safety lever and the grenade would be activated. The M26 grenade was a fragmentation grenade with a four to five second delay time before it would explode. Most likely I wouldn't have time to remove it from my web belt before it went off. I decided to remove them and put one in each of my lower trouser pockets.

The radioman to my left was whispering something to Top. He had heard from the 'point man' about one hundred yards ahead of us. A point man walks ahead of a patrol searching for enemy activity and relays the information back to the radioman and commander. We were signaled through hand motions to crouch real low and maintain silence. We could hear some slight radio chatter in a language I was quickly becoming accustomed to. My left hand was beginning to shake. I squeezed it hard and hid it so it could not be seen. Why just my left hand, I didn't know; perhaps it was because it was my trigger finger hand. I could still feel the sweat from my brow roll into my eyes. It burned like the dickens! I remained still and didn't move to wipe it from my eyes. All I could do was blink to try and clear the sweat. The seconds and minutes seemed to turn into hours. All I could see were green leaves and jungle brush. Then I noticed about a dozen birds ahead of us suddenly take flight. The only times I had seen that happen was when I was hunting in the woods and something spooked them.

About a second later there was a loud blast, a deafening sound I wouldn't soon forget. It wasn't close to me but it was so loud the ground vibrated. Then there was a second blast, and a third. "Take cover!" screamed the corporal. "Damn, they're honing the mortars in on us!" "Where the hell do I take cover?" I uttered to myself. I saw a slight indent in the ground to my right and ran like the dickens to get in it. Someone had started to dig a hole for some reason and hadn't finished it. But I didn't care if it was a latrine hole or what. I was in it and I was going to stay for now. I slowly raised my head to see where the others were. Then I saw the corporal to my left crouched behind a small tree. He glanced at me and put his right index finger to his lips, then pointed straight ahead. It didn't take me long to figure it out. The mortars had stopped and the enemy was heading this way. Silently and slowly, I pointed my M14 frontward and stared down the barrel with my left eye. A thought came to my mind out of nowhere. John Wayne had done the same thing in a Western. He was bearing down on a bad guy with his rifle and one eye staring down the sight. Strange, the things that come into your head at times like that.

Suddenly, there was a "pop" and then another and another. Then all hell broke loose. It was happening! It was really happening! The enemy was out in front. How many, I had no idea. From the sound of the gunfire it could have been a full battalion of Viet Cong. I would find out later that there was only a small squad, but at that moment I didn't care. I didn't have time to think about it. I lifted my rifle, taking no particular aim, and pulled the trigger. Nothing happened. What had been a good thing when I jumped off of the Huey – was a bad thing here. I had never chambered a round. That could have been a costly mistake. I quickly drew back the charging rod and let the round slam forward into the chamber. I began to fire in the direction of the sound. With all the firing going on you never really knew if you actually hit someone. You only found the dead. I had fired off about 60 rounds before I realized it. There were three magazine clips lying on the ground. Each magazine held 20 rounds. The barrel of my rifle was almost red hot.

"Medic! I need a medic over here!" shouted Platoon Sergeant Kearney of the second platoon. Suddenly, a figure appeared about ten yards away doing a hasty low crawl towards Kearney. It was Specialist Walt Frazier. Frazier was a three-year enlistee right out of high school. He came from New York City and was very streetwise. Walt took no guff from anybody. Rumor has it that he'd been associated with a gang and managed to end up before a judge who gave him a choice of two years in jail or the military. It seems Frazier liked to cut up people; the judge figured he might make a good medic. Frazier wasn't too fond of the jail option and decided to take the judge's advice. He enlisted to become a medic. After completing eight weeks of basic training he was sent to Fort Sam Houston in Texas where they trained Army medics. Having finished his combat medical training and after a 30-day leave, Frazier was assigned to the 1st Cavalry Division in An Khe. Frazier and I had met in a mess hall a few days before we left the States. His language was that of a seasoned street fighter. He had a scar about two inches long on the right side of his neck; I figured it was the result of a street fight. When I asked him about it he had laughed. "Nope. I was cutting a box open and the knife slipped." That was all he said. I wasn't convinced. We became friends, but I would never have wanted to cross him.

"Over here, Doc!" Kearney yelled. Frazier made his way to where he saw a soldier writhing in pain. Blood was spurting from his mid-section. Private Kurtz had been in the army for about three months before being sent to Nam. He was a high school dropout and draftee from Kentucky. He had been raised on a farm along with three brothers and two sisters. "My dad always told us that chores were more important than "schoolin." he would say. The poor kid was not very bright. He had to take the Army entrance exams three times before he qualified to enlist, but he was determined to do it. More than anything, he wanted to get away from the farm and drudgery of the same chores day after day, year after year. Patrick Kurtz was not your typical hard-core soldier. He may not have been Harvard-bound, but he had a kindness and gentleness about him. Everyone liked him. Private Kurtz was not a fighter. He wasn't tough. With a slight build, I bet he didn't weigh more than 130 pounds, yet he had muscle strength from working the farm. One thing I knew for sure was that Pat Kurtz was not was a quitter. He was always determined to keep up with the rest of us. We respected him for that.

Crawling out of the hole on my stomach, I made my way over to see if I could help Doc. "Hey, Kurtz, you woke me from a nice nap!" Doc said while sizing up the situation. "Sorry, Doc." he said with his teeth gnashed together. Kurtz was in excruciating pain, yet he was not complaining. As Doc peeled away his shirt and cut the T-shirt up the middle with his scissors, I saw his countenance change in an instant and he swallowed hard. I took a peek at his stomach. "Damn, a gut wound." I whispered under my breath. A gut wound was one of the hardest wounds to dress in the field. Doc flexed Kurtz's knees to prevent further exposure of his abdominal organs. The most you could do was limit the bleeding by covering the wound with a field dressing and call for a Medevac chopper. Sergeant Kearney jumped on the radio and called for one. Time was crucially important with this type of wound.

"Well, Kurtz, you just got yourself a free trip back to the States, you lucky kraut!" Doc uttered. "In country for less than two weeks and you get to go back to the world of round eyes and chicks!" Kurtz's eyes were closed. Doc looked at Kearney and me. We could tell he was trying to hold back tears. He shook his head. We knew what that meant. Tears began to stream down my camouflage-covered face. Half his stomach was gone. Doc quietly, quickly took my right hand and placed it on the left side of the soldier's stomach. As I watched, I saw that Kurtz's intestines were exposed and I was now holding them in. It was all Doc could do to stop Kurtz from bleeding to death right there. Doc wrapped his stomach as best he could. To ease the pain, Doc hit him with a morphine stick. We all carried those in our backpacks just in case.

A few minutes later we could hear the sound of the Medevac chopper coming in from the southeast. We hustled to make a temporary landing area. Cutting away the brush was difficult because we only had our bayonets and one machete. The chopper was coming in and we had to hurry. You never forget the sound of a Huey chopper; "Whump…Whump…Whump." We quickly put Kurtz on a stretcher, and four guys carried him to the chopper. The stretcher was laid crosswise in the Huey and tied down. Then three less-seriously wounded soldiers were put aboard. As the engine and rotors were increasing readying for takeoff, I bent over Kurtz and whispered, "See ya Stateside, Pat!! You'll be in good hands at Walter Reed." He opened his eyes and forced a little grin. The far-away look in his eyes told me he knew the score. I squeezed his hand and backed away. Sergeant Kearney gave a 'thumbs up' to the pilot and the chopper lifted up off the ground and banked towards the 93rd Evac Hospital near Saigon. Kurtz's wound was too serious to take to a Field Aid Station. In our silent thoughts, I think we knew that it was just a matter of time, and so did Private First Class Patrick Kurtz. There would be no Walter Reed Hospital, no stateside meeting with family. There would only be a black body bag, an ID tag and a lousy telegram to Pat's mother and father.

In the midst of all the chaos, I crawled back to my ditch and sobbed like a child. I did what I could to hide my face and not let anyone hear me. Soldiers were not supposed to cry. After all, we were professional soldiers. Emotions were not standard "Army issue." If anyone had told me to stop crying for that kid, I swear I would have hit him with the butt of my rifle. I wasn't a machine or some inanimate object! I was a human being who had a heart that beat every second. With that heart came human emotions, emotions that made you laugh or cry. Pat was my friend. He deserved to have someone cry for him.

Pat was the first combat death I had seen; it would not be the last. You try to hold on to your emotions because emotions mean you are still a functioning individual who has feelings. But after seeing your buddies brutally killed or wounded in combat, you unintentionally let yourself become hardened and distant. You don't want to feel anymore. You begin to shy away from making friends. That becomes your protection. It's safer and much less painful than feeling the emotions. It really stunk, but in the end that's how you survived.

There were more firefights, more patrols in the days ahead. The death toll in our unit had peaked at 16% over the eleven and a half months. It was a hard year, but the days rolled by one by one. Then it was my turn to rotate back home. It would be a bittersweet return to the States. I had survived my tour, but it was accompanied with sadness. In the end, I had lost friends to bullets, sniper fire and mortar. Three of them were close buddies. Another one of those killed was Top. MSG Keworski was hit with shrapnel from a land mine. He had been two weeks away from the end of his tour and was looking forward to retirement after 32 years in the Army and four tours in Nam. He died trying to keep us new guys alive.

CHAPTER EIGHT

DEAD OR ALIVE?

"Sorry, Kate, no mail today." said Mom. Once again I left the room in tears. I would run to my room, throw myself on the bed and bury my head in my pillow so no one would hear me crying. "Why doesn't he write?" I sobbed.

We had pledged ourselves to one another. We had promised to write as often as we could. I had relived the summer we met a thousand times and I know what we felt. I didn't understand why there are no letters. So many things went through my mind. "Is he wounded? Has he been killed?" I asked myself. "Oh, God, please, no!" Every day on the news they would give the daily death count of both the enemy and U.S. soldiers. Every day I would wonder if Mike was one of those. It had been so long since his last letter. I kept it under my pillow. I had read the letter so many times the folds were coming apart. Some of the words were stained with tears.

"How could one short period of time in a single summer turn my heart upside-down?" I thought to myself. I knew the answer; I wasn't fooling myself. In those two brief moments in time, I fell in love with Mike. We had innocently pledged ourselves to one another. A bond was created that was never meant to be broken. But where was he? "Oh God, this is so hard!"

The days turned into weeks. One day, I drove to his parents' home in Weldon Mills. I could tell they were surprised to see me. Mike had told them about me, but we had never met. His mother invited me in. I could tell she wanted to talk. I was disappointed to find they had not heard from Mike in quite awhile either. They had even written the Pentagon, but never heard from them. As I left to go home I told them if I found out anything, I would call them right away. To my surprise, his mom gave me a big hug and promised to do the same. I left them my address and telephone number.

"The local town hall in Weldon Mills might know about Mike," I thought while driving into town. More disappointment. They did not have any updates on Mike.

As I walked out of the town office I noticed a memorial honoring veterans of various wars in front of the building. Listed were the names of those who had lost their lives in WWI, WWII, Korea and the newest names from Vietnam. As I walked around the other side of the memorial I noticed another set of names. There was his name: "Michael D. Thompson." Tears fell, and I began to cry. The town clerk must have heard my sobbing because she came running out of her office towards me. "What's going on?" she asked. By then I had fallen to my knees on the grass, crying uncontrollably. The water in my eyes blurred my vision but I managed to point to Mike's name. My body was shaking and I could feel my heart beating like it was going to burst. The woman gently took my hand, lifted my chin with her other hand and said softly "Honey, the names on this side of the memorial are those from the town who served or are serving in Vietnam." I looked up and stared at her face for what seemed an eternity and then began to cry all over again. But she knew they were not tears of sorrow. I closed my tear-filled eyes, "Thank you, God! Thank you!" This wonderful stranger put her arms around me and hugged me tight for a long time. She knew I needed it that very moment. She smiled and said, "You just keep on looking, honey," as she began walking back into the office. Driving home to Concord, I kept thinking I would find him no matter how long it took. I would never give up.

CHAPTER NINE

CHOPPER DOWN

*T*oward the end of a tour you begin to get nervous about going out on patrols. After all, you've made it through eleven and a half months of your one-year tour. Why risk things now? But in the military you can't pick and choose your missions in war. You go where your superiors send you. My platoon leader had come to me "asking" if I would assist in a recovery operation. A squad of Bravo Company soldiers had been in a firefight. Two soldiers had received serious wounds. They needed to be medevac'd to an aid station. All of the medevac choppers were already out on other missions. Asking me to go was really an order – but it sounded nicer. In the end, I suppose I would have volunteered just the same. After all, they were my brothers.

I was assigned as a door gunner on a Huey chopper. My main weapon was an attached M-60 machine gun on a swiveling mount and a bungee cord to help secure it to the cabin doorway. The gun was a bit bulky but it was also fairly lightweight. I was familiar with this gun having used it on occasion. It was deadly and effective, especially at short distances. You had to carry a spare barrel, as they tended to get hot very quickly. I especially liked the M60.

"Okay, saddle up! We leave in 10 minutes," yelled Captain Dave Engels, my Huey pilot and known as "Cowboy" because of his big Stetson hat. Engels had seen a lot of combat. We always felt confident in his ability to bring us out to the field and back. This was also his last mission before he returned stateside. He was leaving the Army to return to his dairy farm in Nebraska. We were secretly planning a going away party for him, but that would have to wait.

As the chopper lifted off the tarmac, I double-checked my 60 to make sure it was operational. Once away from the take-off pad, I fired a few rounds into the jungle to test it. It performed perfectly. After about 40 minutes Captain Engels yelled, "We hit the LZ in three minutes and it's hot." I knew from experience what that meant. I was ready.

Looking down we could see the U.S. soldiers waiting at the north end of the landing zone. In an instant Engels banked to the left and began a descent. I was secretly wishing he had come in from the other side of the LZ because my 60 was on the right side and pointing in the wrong direction. I couldn't use the gun. "Damn, Captain, you made me useless!! What in hell are you thinking?" I muttered to myself. Carefully making my way to the other side of the ship, I suddenly knew why he was banking left. He had seen what I hadn't; a platoon size group of Viet Cong making their way toward the LZ. They were about 40 yards away. I knew immediately what he was about to do. I could hear Captain Engels talking to the radioman on the ground. He was going to fire some of his rockets into the midst of them. Suddenly, he yelled, "Hold on, gunner!" As I grabbed onto the nearest support pole, I felt the rockets leave the ship and a few seconds later the ground seemed to explode in one enormous fireball. The impact of the rockets and the explosions literally tossed VC bodies into the air in every direction. "That takes care of those fellas," I yelled.

Suddenly I heard a second deafening loud bang and felt the chopper begin to shake violently. "We've been hit! We're going down!" Captain Engels yelled. Somewhere below from the dense jungle, the enemy had managed to fire a rocket-propelled grenade in our direction as we were descending. The chopper began to spiral downward as it headed toward the ground. We were spinning so fast that all I could see was green jungle trees and then the blue sky over and over. I briefly felt the chopper hit the ground and suddenly there was extreme pain on the right side of my head for one split second.

CHAPTER TEN

Northbrook – A Trip Home

I have no memory of how I got to Northbrook Veterans Hospital. The attending nurse said I had been in a coma for quite awhile and then transferred here from Walter Reed Army Hospital. The unit I was in specialized in severe head traumas. I remember seeing a doctor briefly but didn't really recall the conversation we had.

"Hey, soldier, welcome back. Did you have a good nap?" said the nurse. "I wasn't sleeping, I said. I've been trying to remember what happened. Things are all so fuzzy."

"That's not surprising considering what you have been through." I heard her say, as she checked a chart at the foot of my bed.

I struggled to sit up without dislodging the tube connected to my arm. I heard a light tap on the door and watched a doctor enter and move closer to the bed. It was the same doctor I remember talking with earlier. "Let's spend a few minutes together and see where we are," he said. Those few minutes turned into two hours as I told him how far back I could recall and what I remembered before I blanked out. He seemed quite pleased that my memory was returning.

After spending a week with the doctor, and hours in counseling, he said at the end of our last meeting, "I think you are well on the way to recovery and ready for the next step. Considering the serious head wound, you have made great progress. I'll give you a complete physical to make sure the rest of you is in good shape. By the way, I was required to contact the military authorities at Walter Reed when you were able to leave the hospital. Assuming all the tests come out ok, I think we can release you on Friday for transfer back to Walter Reed." As he was leaving the room, I remember thinking how very businesslike this doctor is. I guess it was his way of protecting himself from getting emotionally involved with his patients. That is something I understood well.

"Doctor Goodson, could I have a couple of aspirin? I have a bit of a headache?" "You had a serious head injury. You may have them off and on for awhile," he said. He told the nurse to give me two aspirin.

A few days later, and after a series of physical and mental tests, I was given a clean bill of health. Without delay, I was released from Northbrook and along with other recovering soldiers. We boarded a bus heading to South Station in Boston and then a train to Washington and on to Walter Reed Hospital. About seven hours later we were sitting in a room at the hospital especially for recovering soldiers waiting to be processed. After going through the usual in-processing and more medical evaluations, I was told I was to be given a medical discharge and a 100% disability rating due to the seriousness of the injuries that I had sustained. I thought that strange because except for an occasional headache, I felt healthier than I had in a long time. However, it seems the Army had no further use for a soldier who had sustained a serious head trauma. Even though I was declared healed, the Army didn't want to assume the responsibility if I were to have any subsequent issues while on active duty. So, with my medical discharge papers along with a Bronze Star, Purple Heart, and all of my back pay, I left Walter Reed. For some strange reason, I wasn't too disappointed. I had seen too many of my friends dead or wounded. I had seen enough blood and guts. Not a night went by when I didn't see the face of my dying friend Pat Kurtz. I feel the pain and anguish still. No, I had enough of Vietnam and all of its horror. Maybe that head wound knocked some sense into me, I don't know, but what I did know was I couldn't take any more. The discharge may have been a goodbye to the Army, but the memories would live on.

In a little less than two years, my budding military career was over. But now I had a new mission. I needed to pick up the pieces of my life. I needed to find Kate. We hadn't had contact for a while now. I needed to let my mom and dad know that I am ok, as well. I can only imagine what they are going through. I didn't want to contact them while I was in the hospital and worry them more than they already were.

CHAPTER ELEVEN

THE LIGHT BECKONS

"Mom, what should I do? I haven't heard from Mike for so long! I can't seem to get any answers from the Army. Oh God, something is terribly wrong. I just know it is!" I cried. I knew that my mother had no idea how to go about finding Mike, but I was open to anything she might suggest.

"Honey, I wish I knew what to do. You mustn't think the worst, Kate. At this point the best you can do is to continue to stay busy. That will help you." Mom said.

"Mom, we wrote to each other every day! He was supposed to be home by now. His year was almost up. Mike said in the last letter I got that he had just one last mission to go on and then he would be sent home. He said he would call as soon as he was back."

I briefly raised my eyes and noticed that she had stopped what she was doing and stared at me silently. After a few moments she returned to her work. I could almost read her thoughts. I became frightened and ran into my bedroom. I threw myself onto the bed and began weeping. "No! No! He's OK. I just know he's OK!

Please God, let him be OK! I love him so much!! Please bring him back to me," I prayed. She came into the room and sat on the bed beside me. Mom had never been the type to openly show real emotion. Perhaps it was because of her Irish background and strict upbringing. I didn't know, but at that moment she gently reached for my chin and looked me in the eyes. "Kate, there could be any number of reasons why Mike hasn't contacted you." I knew she meant well but not knowing was so hard. After a gentle embrace she went back to the kitchen.

I knew my mother was right about my needing to keep busy. Otherwise not knowing where Mike was would drive me crazy. Shortly after high school graduation, I had entered a nursing program at a local community college and trained to become a nurse. Because I had taken some nursing courses while I was still in high school, I was able to finish the program ahead of my class. I was fortunate to get a job at a local Veterans hospital. Nursing was difficult, but as hard as it was at times, I enjoyed the work. I felt that I was at least contributing to the recuperation of these wounded soldiers. But it was something else also. I felt maybe I might come across a soldier who knew Mike. Deep inside I realized it was a real long shot, but it kept hope alive. I immersed myself in the work even more as I continued to search for Mike.

I was assigned to the "graveyard shift" from eleven in the evening until seven the next morning. I wasn't crazy about the night shift but as a new nurse, the head nurse thought it was a perfect time for me to learn the ropes and get some experience before I was ready for a day shift.

Northbrook was a large veterans hospital. It consisted of seven buildings. I have yet to visit many of them. I stayed mainly on the fifth floor of Building C, working with soldiers with moderate physical injuries. Because of Vietnam there was certainly no shortage of wounded. There was another trauma unit three buildings away. It is there that the more serious wounded were assigned. Northbrook is the only veterans' hospital in the area, just a thirty-minute drive to work from Concord.

"Kate, would you do me a favor?" asked Sylvia Gleason, the head nurse. Sylvia was about 40 years old and originally from Portland, Maine. She had been a nurse for about 20 years. Even though she was beyond the age of military service, Sylvia volunteered to join the Army. She had applied for an age waiver and because there was a shortage of nurses in the Army, she was approved for a two-year active duty stint. After officer training and a short training time at Fort Sam Houston in Texas, Sylvia was sent to Vietnam. She had worked in a field hospital.

The only time I remember Sylvia speaking about her time in Vietnam was when she was talking to another nurse who had been also there. I overheard them talking about an evacuation hospital in a city named Da Nang. It was where Australian and American wounded were sent. From what I could gather, it was a very hard tour for them both. When her tour was up, she left the military and took a job at Northbrook becoming Head Nurse after a year or so. She knew her job and it showed. Sylvia was very kind and understanding to new nurses like myself. She had the patience to help us along. If we made a mistake, she would show us the proper way to do that particular task. She also expected that we would not repeat the error again. She would often say, "These boys have been through enough and we owe them our best."

"Of course, Sylvia. How can I help?" I said.

"Some patient history charts were sent over here by mistake and they need to go to the Severe Trauma Ward at Building F."

This was a good opportunity to see what the severe trauma unit was like. I put on my coat, picked up the packet of charts and headed out the door. It was about a three-minute walk. I enjoyed getting out of the building for a few minutes. As it was 2:30 a.m., I was glad there were security guards patrolling the hospital grounds. When I entered the building, a security officer asked to see my nursing credentials. " I have never seen you before," he said.

"This is my first visit to this unit. I work over at Building C and am delivering some patient records to the head nurse in the severe head trauma unit." After checking my ID badge, he advised me to go to the third floor and the nurses' station would be through the double doors on the left.

My first impression upon entering the ward was how quiet it was. It was not like my assigned ward, where there was the constant hustle and bustle of nurses and doctors and other health aides. Here, there were numerous patients milling around in the hall talking in low tones. They seemed to stop talking and began to stare at me when I got to the station. I just smiled and began talking to the nurse. Explaining why I was there and handing the charts to the nurse, I asked, "Exactly what type of injuries do you handle on this ward?" I knew a little bit, but wanted to know more.

"Mostly those with extreme severe head trauma," she said. "Soldiers medevac'd from Vietnam are initially sent to Walter Reed Army Medical Center in Washington. Those who need special medical attention because of severe head injuries are sent here. That is our specialty on this ward. Some are more serious than others. Some make it and sadly, some don't. We recently had a soldier who arrived here a while ago in a coma. He had been that way for weeks. He was hurt in a helicopter crash from what I heard. One day out of the blue, he woke up. Startled the dickens out of the attending nurse," she said, laughing.

"I can imagine," I said. "How did that all turn out?"

"Spending a couple of weeks with brain trauma specialists and counselors that handle these kinds of situations helped him and he got a clean bill of health. He was sent back to Walter Reed for out-processing. We believe he is being given a medical discharge due to the seriousness of his injury."

"That's amazing! I love to hear those kinds of success stories. I'm happy for him. Well, I had better get back to my ward. Thank you for sharing that." I said, heading to the elevator.

"Yes, we were so glad to see Sergeant Thompson recover from his wounds." the nurse answered with a big smile.

I stopped dead in my tracks just as the elevator door opened. With no modesty at all, I ran back to the nurse's station. "What did you say his name was?" I asked excitedly.

"Thompson. I just knew they referred to him as Sergeant Thompson. Why?" she wondered.

Not containing my excitement, I asked what his first name was. "Hmmm, let me look. This is not my normal ward so I haven't seen too many soldiers' records on this floor. Let's see. Thompson, Jonathan, Thompson, Marvin... Oh, here it is, Thompson, Michael."

I just stared at the nurse with my mouth opened. "Oh my God! Mike! Oh my God!" I raised my hand to cover my mouth and began to cry. The nurse could immediately see the tears running down my face.

"What's the matter? Are you OK?" she asked quizzically. I am sure I left her quite bewildered because I just said, "I'm fine!" and ran to the elevator.

My heart was beating fast as I ran back to my ward. I ran straight past the security guard without stopping. So many things were going through my head. "It had to be him. It couldn't be chance or simply a man with the same name. It had to be him."

I was out of breath when I got back to the ward. Sylvia saw the state I was in. The tears, the red face and my heavy breathing all said something was amiss. "What on earth is going on with you? Are you feeling OK, Kate?"

"He was here, Sylvia! He was here all the time on the Severe Head Trauma ward!" I managed to say.

"You're telling me that your boyfriend was in Building F?"

"Yes, but they just transferred him to Walter Reed! The nurse in F said he was going to be medically discharged! He's alive, Sylvia!"

Hearing the excitement in my voice, she said, "Tell you what, Kate. Finish your shift and take three or four days vacation leave. I will call a substitute nurse in your place. Go, find your man."

It was all I could do to finish my shift. It seemed like it took forever, but finally at 7:20 a.m. and after numerous patient charts were updated, I bolted out the door to tell my Mom and Dad.

"Oh, Kate, are you sure this could be the same Michael Thompson? I would hate to have you disappointed." Dad warned softly.

"I don't know how I know it's him, but I just know!! It's such a deep, unexplainable feeling, Dad! I am going to use some vacation time and go to D.C. to find him. He was sent to Walter Reed Army Medical Center. I got permission from my head nurse to take a few days off."

The next day, I took a train from Boston to New York and transferred to one headed to Washington. This trip was taking most of my savings, but I didn't care. Mike was my whole world and I was going to find him no matter how much it cost. As the train pulled out of the station, I closed my eyes and began to think of what I would say when I found him. I knew I would smile with joy and then begin to cry. But it would be a happy cry if there was such a thing. I would jump into his arms and squeeze him as tight as I could. I would never let go.

CHAPTER TWELVE

THE RETURN

efore I could begin to look for Kate, I needed to go home to my folks. I hadn't called them from the hospital because my mother was a real worrier. I knew they would already be very concerned because they hadn't heard from me and I didn't want to increase their anxiety by mentioning I was in a hospital. I didn't know if the military had contacted them or not by now. In a time of war, things like this can easily slip by.

"Oh, my goodness, Mike, where are you?" my Mom yelled into the phone.

"I'm on my way home, Mom." I said calmly. I'll be there tomorrow afternoon. Are you and Dad OK?"

"Mike, we've been so worried. We have not had any information about you in a long time. We didn't know where you were, son," my Dad said to me from the phone in the den.

"I'll explain it all when I get home. Just know that I am fine," I said.

"Mike, that young lady Kate you told us about was here a while ago." Mom said, as I started to hang up the phone. "She said she has been searching for you a long time. Oh Mike, she seems like such a nice girl. And she is so worried. I could tell that she loves you very much."

"She's the most wonderful girl in the world, Mom." I replied.

After a very few hours of rest at a local motel, I took a taxi to the nearest car rental agency and rented a car. I must have broken every speed limit along the way, but I was anxious to get home.

Even before I got out of the car, I could see my mother rushing out of the front door and down the steps of the porch. She was not an outwardly emotional person, but she had her arms wrapped around me before I had a chance to shut the car door. Dad came out a second later and shook my hand. "Welcome home, Son," was all he said with a slight smile.

Over coffee and Mom's wonderful apple pie, I explained what had happened. There was no reason to go into some of the gory aspects of my time in 'Nam, so I watered it down a quite bit. We talked for about two hours. I am not sure they totally understood all that I had said. They were not interested in all that happened. They were simply glad I was home, safe and sound.

"I just remembered I have something you should see," Mom said, jumping up. A minute later she came out with a small shoebox. "These are letters you never received. We got all of these in the mail about two weeks ago. They were all bundled up. There was no explanation or anything. We wrote them awhile back but never received an answer. We were so frightened that we eventually called the Pentagon! They said they had no record where you were listed as a casualty. Even they didn't know why the mail never got delivered. They promised to investigate."

"Don't hold your breath." I didn't say this out loud but there was no way the Pentagon was going to put much effort into finding out why mail never reached it destination. I told them it didn't matter now, and they both agreed. They were as happy to see me as I was to see them.

I was anxious to find Kate, but it had been a long day and I was really exhausted. The last few weeks had finally caught up with me. I asked Mom if she would make me her famous spaghetti dinner. With a big smile she headed into the kitchen. She knew that was my favorite meal.

After dinner, I showered and went to my old bedroom. Nothing much had changed. It was as if I had only been away for a day or two. Somehow, I found that comforting. Pictures of Elvis, Connie Francis and Bobby Rydell were still on the wall where I had taped them when I was a freshman in high school. That all seemed so silly and so long ago. I guessed that's what war did to me; or maybe it was because I had simply grown up.

I was awakened by sunlight peeking through the window shade. Glancing at the clock on the night table, I took note of the time, 10:30. I must have drifted off right away because I had fallen asleep on top of the blankets all night. As I lay there, thoughts of Kate began to consume me. I decided I would head to Concord and look for her.

Concord was about a ninety-minute drive from Weldon Mills. The quickest way to get there was to take Route 2 east.

In my excitement to get going, I forgot that I had no civilian clothes and I was not about to wear my Army uniform. The Vietnam War had become very unpopular in America and we had been advised to wear civilian clothes whenever possible. Besides, I was a civilian now!

I told my Mom, who understood my dilemma, "I don't want to have to go to the local clothing store and spend time picking out clothes."

"Well, I just happen to have all of your clothes in the spare bedroom closet," Mom said. "I left them there knowing you would be back home."

"Thanks, Mom. By the way, do you have any aspirin? I have this headache. Most likely from all the travel and excitement," I said.

I found some clothes I could wear. I was not the skinny kid that left home. Time and training had altered my body. The shirt and slacks were a bit tight, but I couldn't have cared less. "Thanks Mom, you always were so efficient."

I don't know when I'll be back. Probably in a day or two." I said with a big smile as I darted out of the house and hopped into the car. I know they would have liked me to stay home longer but they could see my excitement in trying to find Kate.

The closer I got to Concord, the more excited I became, yet the same old questions were dancing around in my head. "Will she still feel the same? Did she give up and find someone else?" I couldn't help thinking how long it had been since we last heard from each other. Time and separation can do strange things. And if her mail had been returned to her, I could only imagine what she must have been thinking.

CHAPTER THIRTEEN

ON TO WASHINGTON, D.C.

As the train pulled into Union Station, my heart began to beat rapidly. Anxiety and nervousness were beginning to set in. It had been so long ago since we last were together. "Had I changed," I wondered? "Had Mike changed? Did he still feel the same?"

"Union Station!" the conductor called. I quickly got my bag and headed to the doorway of the car. As I stepped off the train all I could see were people going here and there. Everyone seemed to be in a great rush. Folks were bumping into one another making their way to the train car I had just left. A number of times, I was jostled as I tried to find my way to an information booth. I had no idea how I was going to get to Walter Reed.

Looking around, I suddenly spotted a man in uniform. His left leg was in a cast and he was walking with crutches. Maybe he would know how to get to the hospital. "Excuse me, I wonder if you might be able to help me? I'm trying to get to Walter Reed Hospital. Could you direct me?" I boldly asked the soldier.

He was very kind and gave me directions on how to get there.

DAVID V. SMITH

He said that it would be easiest to take a bus. The soldier pointed to a kiosk where he said I could buy tickets. I was quickly able to get directions from the woman in the Kiosk and bought the bus ticket I needed.

It seemed to take forever, but the bus finally stopped in front of a huge building with a large sign, "Walter Reed Army Medical Center." It was an enormous brick building with lots of windows. People were constantly going in and out of what appeared to be the main door. As I walked up the steps, I became more and more excited. Entering the building, I saw even more people all hurrying with a purpose. I saw lots of men and women wearing white uniforms with stethoscopes around their necks. There were also ordinary people milling around. Some were simply sitting in chairs. A few were walking around and stopping to glance at the various pictures on the walls telling of Walter Reed's history. Other medical staff personnel were pushing carts carrying supplies. There was no doubt, it was a busy place.

Regaining my focus, I was able to find an information booth. After telling the lady at the desk my purpose for being there, she directed me to the Admissions Desk. I explained to the woman in Admissions that I was looking for a soldier named Mike Thompson who had been sent recently from Northbrook in Massachusetts. Searching her records, she said, "Yes, we admitted a Sergeant Michael Thompson recently. He was assigned to the Medical Evaluation Unit."

"Do you think I could see him?" I asked excitedly. "I have come so far." She could see that I was getting more and more anxious.

"Let me call upstairs," she kindly answered. All I could do was to close my eyes and cross my fingers. I was about to burst with excitement. I couldn't hear her talking on the phone as she was speaking in a really low voice. A moment later she hung up the phone and looked up at me.

"Sergeant Thompson's evaluation was completed and he was discharged this morning. I'm sorry, honey, but you missed him by a couple of hours."

She could see my face fall, but couldn't add anything. I did my best to hide the tears. I thanked her and rushed out the door and sat on the nearest bench. I needed to think. "What do I do now?" I cried to myself. After a few moments, I decided I would simply take the train back to Boston and return home. I was extremely tired, but I needed to get back quickly. Once again, I headed on the bus to Union Station. I would catch the next train back no matter what time it was, even though it would be quite late.

It seemed like an eternity returning on the train. There were endless stops. I eventually got a seat by a window. I enjoyed looking at all of the passing scenery. It helped to clear my mind. The movement of the train made me sleepy yet, I was too anxious to sleep. I was deep in thought when an older lady sat down in a recently vacated seat beside me. She was very talkative, but I didn't mind because that helped to pass the time. She said she had been visiting a friend in Arlington who had been recently widowed. In the midst of the conversation she took out some yarn and knitting needles and began knitting as she talked. She asked me where I was heading.

"I'm going back home to Massachusetts. I came to Washington to see a friend of mine who was wounded in Vietnam, but I found out he was discharged earlier today," I said. I think she figured out almost instantly that it was more than just a friend. The sadness in my voice was quite apparent, but I couldn't help myself.

"Is he your boyfriend, honey?" she asked. I nodded yes. "He has been away so long and was wounded from a helicopter crash and we haven't had contact for quite a while." I blurted out, beginning to cry.

She put her knitting down and turned her head towards me

and took my hand in hers. "Honey, I know how you must feel. My late husband was in World War II and he was gone for over three years. He was with General Patton when Patton blasted though France and Germany. I must have worried a million tears. I didn't hear from him for weeks and sometimes months at a time. I didn't know where or if he was. And wouldn't you know... one day he comes walking into the house just as if he had been in the back yard mowing grass. I ran and hugged him 'til he could hardly breathe. And then I pounded his chest so hard for scaring me like that. But he was all smiles."

"He's gone now." she continued. "My Johnny died three years ago. He's buried in Arlington National Cemetery," she said, while looking out the window. "I miss him so much. But we made the best of those years we had together. Two sons and four grandchildren."

Somehow that story made me feel so much better. Mike was home from Vietnam and he was alive, I kept thinking. I should be grateful for that and not feel sorry for myself.

"Honey, you keep trying to find him. I just know you will. I can see the love in your eyes and hear it in your voice," she said, as she picked up her needles and began knitting.

The train pulled into Boston around 11:30 p.m. that night. I was tired and hungry. I realized I hadn't eaten other than a bagel and coffee early that morning. But I decided I would forget about eating and headed straight to the bus terminal nearby. I had just enough money to buy a ticket back to Concord. I made a collect call home and asked Dad if he would meet me at the bus station. He didn't seem to mind that it would be really early in the morning before he got back to bed. At least he didn't show it. Dad and I always had a nice father and daughter relationship. He put up with a lot when I was younger, yet he was always patient with me and mostly understanding.

After about 45 minutes, Dad pulled up to the curb and I hopped into the car. "Kitten, you look exhausted," he said.

"I am, Dad. But mostly I'm disappointed that I missed Mike in Washington. Tomorrow I'll figure out what to do, but right now I'm hungry and tired."

Knowing that I would be tired and hungry, Mom had made a pot of Irish beef stew, one of my favorite dinners. While eating, I explained how I had missed Mike by a few hours. They didn't ask a lot of questions, but simply listened. After finishing the stew, I said that I really needed to get to bed. I also knew that Dad had to get up early and go to work. It was already 2:30 in the morning.

I had no trouble falling asleep. When I finally awoke it was 12:30 in the afternoon. Dad was at work and Mom was hanging out clothes in the back yard.

"Well, good afternoon, Kate. I hope you slept well," she said. "There is coffee on the stove and some pastries in the breadbox. What are you plans for today?"

I hadn't really put much thought to what I would do next.

CONCORD

*I*t was a bright sunny day and except for a bit of a headache, I was feeling great. I was almost to Concord. Once again, my heart was beating fast. It was almost like the first time Kate and I had met at the park. I was thinking about what I would say to her. I decided to simply wait and see. I knew the words would come.

As I turned the corner onto Wellington Street I could see the old farmhouse. Kate had described it so many times, it was as if I had been there before. I looked around at the neighborhood and thought how strange it was for a farmhouse to be settled in the middle of what seemed to be an upscale community. Of course, like most old New England towns, this was once a large farming community and this home may be all that remains of a past era. There was a fairly large apple tree to the right of the house. I could see two small birch trees on the front lawn along with a slew of dandelions. Most people considered them a nuisance but I liked them. Kate knew that. To the left of the house and a bit to its rear was an old barn with the remnants of a silo long since gone. Kate had mentioned in a letter that her father liked to restore old cars and the barn was where he did the work. The white '64 Mustang her parents had given her the summer after we met was the result of one of his rebuilt restorations.

As I pulled into the driveway, excitement and anxiety overwhelmed me. The Mustang was sitting in the driveway, alongside of a black Ford coupe. Stepping out of the car, I very quietly shut the door. Praying she was home, I wanted to really surprise her. Just as I began to walk up the numerous steps leading to the front door things went black for a moment and I became a little dizzy. It went away almost as quick. I was glad of that. Probably just the excitement of the moment, I figured.

The front door had an old-fashioned doorknocker in the shape of a woodpecker. Quite nervously, I gave it a couple of knocks. In response, I heard footsteps. I swallowed hard as the door slowly opened. The sweat on my hands was dripping so I quickly wiped them on my slacks.

Mrs. Flynn stared at me for what seemed like an eternity. "Oh my goodness!!" Kate's mother said covering her mouth with her hand. "I can't believe it! Come in! We have been so worried about you! Kate has been frantic to find you!" Even though she had only seen me twice and not for a little over two years, she knew who I was. She quickly ushered me into the living room. "Mike, Kate is upstairs. She has had a few very busy days, but she will tell you about that I'm sure."

"Mom, who was that knocking at the door?" Kate yelled from upstairs.

As she came down the stairs with a hairbrush in her right hand, brushing halfway down her beautiful blonde hair, she suddenly stopped and stared. For a moment, it was as if time stood still. There was no movement from any of us. We just gazed at one another. Suddenly, Kate dropped the brush and ran down the stairs. "Mike!" she cried. She literally jumped into my arms, squeezing me tight. She began to cry into my shoulders. I could see her mother standing there not knowing what to do. Suddenly, she smiled and said she needed to do something in the kitchen.

"Oh Mike, kiss me! Hold me tight! I want us to remember this moment forever!" Kate said with tears running down her face. I had tears as well. We stood in the front hall for a long time just holding on to one another. The warmth of her kiss and the tightness of her arms around me erased much of the recent past, at least for the moment.

I asked Kate if we could sit down for a few minutes. As we sat on the couch, her mother came into the living room and asked if we'd like some coffee. She sat down with us for a while as Kate and I explained events of the last few months. We talked for a long time, our eyes constantly on the other.

Just around dinnertime, Kate's father came home from work. It was so nice to see him again. He had a subdued look, but that changed when he saw the joy on Kate's face. "Well, Mike! I'm happy to see you back safe and sound! Now maybe I can get a full nights sleep," he chuckled while looking at Kate and giving her a wink. During dinner we updated Kate's father.

A while later, Kate and I decided to go for a walk. We wanted to be alone. She drove me to a park where there was a walking path. The path was the same one that the American soldiers had retreated on during the Battle of Lexington in 1775. Hand in hand, we walked and talked, stopping every few steps to behold one another and hug as hard as we could. We stopped and leaned against a railing on the famous North Bridge that crossed the Concord River. We stood there in silence with our arms around each other. There were people walking around as well, but we didn't care if they stared at us. They didn't know our story.

"Mike, I never doubted we would meet again, and here we are in a park, just like when we first met," Kate said. "But I began to worry when the letters stopped. I had weak moments when

I thought you were gone from me forever. But I never gave up. Oh, Baby, it was such a horrible time not knowing. Every day the news was telling us about the number of men killed and I couldn't help wondering if you were one of them. It was awful, Mike. I couldn't understand why I wasn't hearing from you." I told her about the mail screw-ups and how crazy things like that happen during war.

"Let's put that all behind us, Kate and look to the future," I said. We continued to walk, but in blissful silence.

CHAPTER FIFTEEN

AHEAD

*O*ver the next few weeks, Kate and I began to plan for the future. Being old school, I asked her father and mother for permission to marry their daughter and they both said yes. I think they figured they might not have a real choice in the matter, as they knew the love Kate and I shared. It was decided we would have a July wedding. That was the month we had first met back in '65. It seemed hard to believe that was almost three years ago.

Kate suggested I consider going to college and she would continue to work at Northbrook. I knew that my 100% disability along with the GI Bill for education would allow me to go to school. With Kate working and my government benefits, we would be fine until I graduated. I applied and was accepted at the University of Massachusetts for the Fall semester. I couldn't believe how well things were going for Kate and me after what we had been through.

With the wedding a little over two months away, I decided to get a job, at least until the semester began in September. Kate put me in touch with the groundskeeper at Northbrook who happened to be looking for a temporary man to help with summer mowing and general yard work. Northbrook VA covered a large area and much of it was grass, with lots of bushes and trees. Greg Jackson, the man who oversaw the grounds, asked if I had any physical reasons why I couldn't perform mowing tasks. "No, sir," I said. 'I have headaches once in awhile, but that's all." That didn't seem to faze him and he said I could begin on Monday. Greg knew that Kate and I were to be married in July and he had no problems with my taking the time off. He said that I could take 10 days off for the wedding. I knew that was a busy time but he said, "After all you and Kate have been through, you deserve the time together." Greg didn't share much of his personal life, and it was only later that I found out Greg had a son in Vietnam.

Kate and I spent the next weekend with her parents planning the wedding. We decided not to have a fancy wedding. A simple ceremony at the park where we met and a small reception in Weldon Mills was agreeable to the four of us. As for a wedding trip, we thought it would be wonderful to simply rent a cabin in the park. We were fortunate to find a vacancy that time of year thanks to a cancellation. It was ironic that the cabin was the same one that her parents had rented the summer we met. A week after the wedding, George and Colleen would return with their tent and camp.

Monday morning I began my new job. My first assignments were to mow the grass and trim around hedges. As the days went by, Greg slowly had me doing more. My latest task was to cut down some overhanging branches from a tree close to a doorway leading into the administration building. Greg was concerned that one of the branches could snap off and hurt someone. It was a very old New England maple tree with numerous dead branches.

I headed up the ladder about 12 feet and began sawing away at the branches. The first two small branches went down with no problem; however, the third branch was a bit tougher and I began to saw harder and harder. There was a knothole that I needed to get through. My arms were getting tired and I could feel a headache coming back. I kept on sawing until I was finally able to knock the branch off with the help of an axe. The pain in my head was worse so I decided to get some of the aspirin I kept in my lunch bag. As I started down the ladder, I felt myself getting dizzy. My eyes began to get blurry. I started to wonder what was happening. Was it the sun and heat exhaustion? I could feel the blood in my head pulsing rapidly. I knew something wasn't right so I decided to head over to the nurse's office. Then I noticed it was getting dark.

Kate was still working her shift when she got a call, "Kate, this is Greg. I need you to come to the Emergency Room now. Mike was cutting some branches and another worker saw him fall to the ground. The doctor is with him."

"Oh God, no!" I screamed in my head. "This can't be happening!! It's not fair! Please God! He has been through so much! You can't let anything happen to him!" I couldn't stop crying.

Rushing to the ER, I was escorted to a curtain-walled room where Mike was. At first, all I could see were monitors and tubes. I was used to seeing these things, but not on someone I loved so deeply. Mike had his eyes closed and looked quite calm, as if he were taking a nap. I took his hand and sat down in the chair beside the bed while I waited for the doctor or nurse to give me some information.

"Mike, I whispered, I know you can hear me. I don't know what's wrong Baby, but we can get through this." I need you. You are my life. I love you so much! Fight, Baby, fight." I said squeezing his hand tightly.

A few minutes later, the doctor came in. I had known Dr. Dennis Atwater for about a year. He came to the ward where I worked every so often. He was a military surgeon and had a great reputation in his field. I was pleased to see him.

"Kate, Mike has had a relapse. Apparently the head injury he suffered in the helicopter crash never fully healed. We think his working on the tree limbs may have aggravated it. I was told by another groundskeeper who saw Mike fall that he seemed a bit dizzy just before he fell off the ladder."

"Doctor Atwood, Mike has been complaining of headaches. But he hasn't paid too much attention to them and has been taking aspirin."

"We're going to take Mike for an X-ray to see what's going on. As soon as I know anything, I will get back to you, Kate. I promise."

As Mike was being wheeled out of the room, I bent over and kissed him. "Hang tough, my brave soldier. I'll be here when you wake up, Baby. I love you so much!"

I knew there was a chapel nearby, so I headed there. I wanted to be alone. So many thoughts were going through my head. "What if this...what if that...?" In the small chapel I could be away from all of the hospital noise. As I knelt down in the pew closest to the altar, I could see a huge cross on the wall. As always, Jesus was hanging on the cross, but this time it seemed different. Before, it had just been an icon to me. Of course, with my Catholic upbringing I knew what it all meant, but at this moment the Man on the cross became so real. I sensed a closeness I had never really felt before. Looking up and staring into Jesus's eyes, it was as if He were saying, "Speak to me, Kate."

"Lord, you know how much I love Mike. And you know how much he has gone through. Please don't take him. You know how much I need him," I prayed. I sat there quietly for what seemed like an eternity. "He is my whole world, God. We've been apart for so long. I know we are meant to be together. Please don't let it end like this, please!" I sat back in the pew and closed my eyes.

Suddenly, I realized I needed to call Mike's parents and let them know what was going on. Finding a pay phone outside one of the waiting rooms, I talked with Mike's mother. Trying to minimize her fears as best I could, I assured her of an update with any news. She said she and her husband would come out to the hospital as soon as they could.

After awhile I went back to the ER but found they had moved Mike to a patient room. I wondered if that was a good sign. I found Mike about the same as when he was downstairs: tubes, monitors and all. I had decided during my quiet time in the chapel that I would not allow myself to prepare for the worst. We had not come through war, a helicopter crash and a long period of separation to have it all end here. I would not leave his side until he woke up.

An hour or so later, Dr. Atwood came in and sat down next to me. "We have the results of the X-ray. The headaches appear to be caused by pressure on the brain. The strenuous activity of cutting off the tree limbs may have increased the pressure to a point where the pain was so great, he became dizzy, passed out and fell off the ladder. We are going to go in and try to release the pressure but that will mean…."

"I know, Dr. Atwood. You will need to cut into his skull. I'm aware how serious an operation that can be." I said to him. "I realize it's tricky, but I know you will do all that you can."

"We have scheduled the operation as soon as he is prepped."

After Dr. Atwood left, I immediately called Mike's Mom and Dad and told them the doctor wanted to do the operation this afternoon. His Mom said they would drive out in about an hour, as soon as his Dad got off of work.

Back in the room, I sat down and held Mike's hand. I could hear his breathing and could see his chest move up and down. Again, I began talking to him as if he were awake. "Mike, we have more wedding plans to make. My wedding dress is almost done. You need to decide what you want to wear. When you wake up we will talk about these things." I didn't really know if he could hear me or not. I have heard so many stories of people saying they could hear what was being said. I believed them and felt in my heart and mind that Mike knew what I was saying.

"I love you, Mike. I have since the first time we met at the park. Do you remember meeting at the concession building? I remember how awkward you were. So much has happened since that summer. I want you to fight hard and come back to me. I will be here every minute until you wake up. You came out of one coma and you can come out of this one. I need you, Michael Thompson! Oh, Mike, please hear me! I don't want to live my life without you. I can't, I just can't!"

At some point, being so tired and stressed, I fell into a chair and drifted off to sleep, only to be awakened by a nurse who said they were going to prep Mike for the operation. Being a nurse, I knew what that meant. Not wanting to be in the way, I headed to the hospital cafe for a coffee. Having been with Mike for quite a while, I remembered I had not eaten or had anything to drink. The coffee tasted so good along with a buttered croissant. I could feel myself regaining some strength.

As I sat with the coffee and pastry, suddenly I saw Tom Davis, Mike's best friend from high school walking in. I just stared at him and couldn't move. I had not seen Tom for quite awhile. As he came over to me, I jumped up and suddenly began crying. He did not say anything and just put his arms around me and held me close for what seemed like an eternity. I needed those moments so much. I had been holding myself together for Mike, but seeing Tom I just let out all the feelings I had been holding back. "Oh, Tom!" is all I could say while fighting back the tears.

"I just got word about Mike. I'm so sorry, Kate. I had no idea what had happened to Mike. We'd lost touch for quite a few months. Just by chance, I decided to stop by his parents' house to try and find him and they told me all that had been going on.

I guess I saw them just after you talked to his mother. I hopped in the car and came here. They said he was busy with medical people so I couldn't see him right then. One of the nurses said that his wife was here but left. I just knew it was you. I took a chance that you might be either here or the chapel," Tom said.

I couldn't help but smile. "Well, Mike and I are not married yet. We were making plans when this happened. We are planning a July wedding at the park where we met. By the way, Mike was going to ask you to be his best man. He was about to start tracking you down." I said. "It is so good to see you, Tom," I continued. "You are just what I needed today. This is so hard. Mike apparently was not fully healed from his helicopter crash and had a relapse after doing some strenuous yard work. The doctor is going to open his skull and try to relieve the pressure causing the pain."

"Kate, does it happen to be a Doctor Atwood?" Tom asked.

"Yes, he visits the ward I work on regularly. Have you heard of him? He has a good reputation here."

"Dr. Atwood is the best surgeon around. My father is a World War 2 vet and Dr. Atwood operated on him a few years ago. Tom said. "He has a great record for successful operations like this one."

I know Tom was trying to put me at ease and there was so much truth to what he was saying. He didn't realize how much he was helping me cope. He was going to stay with me until Mike was out of the operation. Up until then, I had wanted to be alone, but now I was glad he was there.

After awhile, Tom and I went back to Mike's room. By now he had been prepped and was lying there all covered except for his head. It was hard to look at his head. They had shaved a portion of it where they were about to operate. I kept telling myself it would grow back.

"Time to go," the nurse said as she entered the room. Two

aides came in and began unhooking tubes and getting the bed ready to be moved to the operating room.

"Wait a second, please!" I said as I leaned over the bed and gently kissed Mike's lips. "I love you, Mike. I'll be here when you get back. Come back to me, baby," I whispered as I gave his hand a little squeeze and kissed his forehead.

CHAPTER SIXTEEN

COME BACK TO ME

om was sitting beside me holding my hand. There was not much conversation. The waiting room for family and friends always seemed to be a quiet place. Two small children were calmly coloring in some coloring books. Watching them fill in the pages with bright, cheery colors made me smile. As I looked around the room, I could see the silent worry on the faces. We pretty well knew what each was thinking. Time seemed endless. Every so often, a doctor would come into the room and ask a person or family to follow him to his office. I knew that our time would come eventually.

About two hours or so later, as I was thumbing through a magazine, I heard, "Hi, Kate," from a quiet, familiar female voice. "Do you mind some company for a while?" It was my Mom and Dad. They both gave me a big hug. It was so comforting. It was more meaningful to me, as Dad was not an overly demonstrative person and generally was not a hugger.

"Oh, of course not. I'm so glad to see you." I replied. "Do you remember Mike's friend, Tom Davis?"

"It's been a couple of years," said Tom smiling. "Good to see you again. I'm sorry it has to be under these circumstances."

"Mike is in the operating room now. He's been there a little over two hours. The doctor said it would take between three and five hours depending on the seriousness. It could be longer," I said.

"Your Dad and I have been at the church praying for you and Mike. Father O'Callaghan is lighting a prayer candle for him," Mother said as she took my other hand. "We know how hard this is for you, Kate."

"That's really nice of Father O'Callaghan. And thank you both. I am so glad you are here. Tom has been with me since Mike was taken into the operating room. He has been like a big brother to me," I said smiling at Tom.

We talked for quite a while. We had not seen Tom for a long time, and I asked him what he had been up to. He mentioned traveling overseas after his graduation from high school. He had spent a few months traveling in Germany and France. He only came home because his mother was quite ill. She had passed away two weeks after Tom returned home.

"I've decided to remain in the States and get a regular job. When I finished school, I tried to go into the military but because of my diabetes I was ineligible. All my friends were either getting drafted or enlisting, so I thought I would as well. I knew I had a slim chance, but I wanted to try anyways. That rejection bothered me so much that I had to leave the States. I couldn't face my friends who served," Tom said.

"But Tom, you tried. It wasn't your fault. I respect you for that!" I said. "No one would blame you."

"I agree with Kate, Tom. You did your best to get into the military and that's what counts," my Dad said. "If you had run away to Canada or someplace to avoid the draft, I would feel different, but you tried. There is honor in that you tried."

A few minutes later during a quiet moment, I heard a woman's voice, "May we wait with you?" It was Mike's mother and father standing just outside the doorway. "Oh my goodness, of course, please, come in. I'm so glad you are here. I stood to embrace them both and introduced them to everyone. "Mike has been in surgery for quite awhile now so we should know something soon," I said.

"We're not used to driving far so it took awhile to find the hospital," Mike's mother said.

"No, I'm very happy you came. I know how hard it must be for you," I said.

They hadn't sat down for two minutes when the doctor entered the room. "Kate, would you and your family come into my office?" said Dr. Atwood.

I froze and stared at him. It was the most fearful moment of my life. I slowly raised myself from the chair, all the while not taking my eyes off Dr. Atwood. Once again my heart began pounding so fast I thought it would burst. I took Tom's hand and held onto it. Tom wasn't family, but I wanted him there. I was glad that both our parents were here. We needed each other's support.

Sitting at his desk, Dr. Atwood stared at some papers he had in his hand. His face showed no emotion at all. I was beginning to get worried. My heart was pumping blood so rapidly. I was holding back tears as I quickly introduced him to everyone. "Please, say something!" I screamed to myself.

"When we removed part of Mike's skull, we found a mass of abnormal cells pressing against his brain. That was causing Mike's headaches. Our best guess is that the mass had something to do with the injury he received in Vietnam. Apparently, he was taking the aspirin to ease the pain, but the strenuous activity with his work caused the mass to enlarge. Medical science is not exact in certain areas, so we cannot really define the cause, but all roads lead us to that conclusion. However, the good news is that his mass was not malignant and we were able to remove it successfully. Given a couple of weeks Mike will be fine. However, I want to keep him here for observation a few days and then send him home."

I began to cry. This time I cried really hard. I must have let out all the pent-up emotions I had inside. Tom and my parents surrounded me and hugged me. It must have been quite a sight! I could see great relief on Mike's parents' faces, too. "Take a few minutes to relax. I can imagine the stress all this has caused, but the outcome is the best we could have hoped for. Mike will be back in his room in about four hours. I am very happy for you all," Dr. Atwood said with a smile as he left his office.

We all headed to Mike's room to wait until he was out of recovery. Mom could see that I was emotionally exhausted, and suggested I take a nap in the chair next to the bed. She knew I would not go home to rest. I knew I needed to rest and took her advice. But first I said I needed to go to the chapel for a few minutes. Knowing I would need time alone, they headed to the coffee shop on the first floor.

As I knelt down in the front pew, I looked again at the cross bearing Jesus' body. As the tears rolled down my cheeks, I whispered, "Oh dear Jesus, thank you for bringing Mike back to me. Thank you for not taking him away. I promise I will take care of him always."

CHAPTER SEVENTEEN

A Summer in Time

When I got back to the room, everyone was there. It had been a long day and it was decided that they would go out to dinner. There was no way on earth I was going to leave Mike's bedside. They understood that and besides, I was not the least bit hungry. A couple of minutes later, I was alone in the room waiting.

I must have been in a deep sleep curled up in the chair because when I awoke, Mike was back in the room and seemed to be resting comfortably. He was still attached to the various monitors. I could see the heart monitor showing every beat and was so happy to see that. It was a strong beat and regular. Moving the chair closer to his bed, all I could do was hold his hand and stare at his face. I didn't mind that his head was bandaged or that he had tubes in his arm. He was alive and that was all I cared about. These moments were Mike's and mine. I was glad no one was in the room and when he woke up, he would see me first. I was so happy the others decided to wait in the waiting room after having dinner.

In the middle of a Reader's Digest story, my eyes caught a slight movement. Mike was beginning to stir. I could see him blinking his eyes and slowly looking around. He turned his head gently and saw me. We both smiled at the same time. I reached for his hand and squeezed it. He gently squeezed back. Once again, I began to cry.

"You can't imagine how beautiful you look to me," Mike said softly. "And by the way, I will figure out what I will wear at our wedding. I heard you, Kitten. I heard everything you said."

"You look gorgeous to me, Baby." I said with tears again running down my cheek. That was all I could say at that moment."

Five days later, Mike was discharged from the hospital. I had him stay in the extra bedroom in our house until he felt stronger. I would nurse him back to health. Mom and Dad were not too sure that was a good idea, but did not object. A week later Mike felt good enough to return to his own room at his parent's house. I was able to drive him to Weldon Mills as it was a Saturday and I was off work for the weekend. His mother was taking good care of him. He had begun to wear a baseball cap to hide the small bandage that was left. He was sensitive to his lack of hair. I assured him it made no difference to me and reminded him that it would grow back. Mike was pretty well back to normal after three weeks. He was driving back and forth to Concord every couple of days now.

Mike was not going back to his job at the hospital. It was decided he would simply prepare for the wedding and the college semester in September. However, I had to go back to work. The hospital generously granted me extra leave time but it had been with no pay. I was glad to return to work with the wedding coming soon.

Mike and I went about planning the wedding. Mom and Dad were getting nervous about all the details that needed to be done in time. We would simply smile at one another. After what we had gone through since the summer of '65, nothing caused us great concern.

Taking a stroll hand in hand one evening at a small park in Concord, we sat down on the grass with our arms around each other in total silence. We stared at a little pond and watched a family of ducks slowly paddling across to the other side all lined up one after the other. Kate had her eyes closed and a little smile on her face.

"Can you believe we are here, Kate?" I whispered. "Can you believe that in three days we will be standing in front of the concession stand where we first met saying our wedding vows?"

She looked at me with a huge smile. I gave her a quizzical look. "Why the big smile," I asked.

"I'm smiling because my folks cannot understand why we don't have a regular church wedding like others. 'Why drive all the way out there?" Mom said to me. "She is still so old fashion in some ways," Kate said.

"I knew from the moment we met at the park that very first time that you were the one I was going to love. You were the one I would marry. Don't ask me how I knew but I felt it, and that feeling has never gone away. I want to tell you something I never mentioned before. One night just before you left for the Army, Dad came to my room and sat down on the bed."

Taking my hand he said quietly, "Kate, you know that Vietnam is building up and that Mike is a prime candidate to be sent there. They are sending so many there. Are you sure you want to get involved with a young man with an uncertain future? You could be in for some real hurt and I wouldn't want you to go through that."

"I know, Dad. I've thought about that. But there is something between us that was meant to be. I really believe it, and so does Mike. We have talked this all out. We know that things can happen, but we are willing to take the risk." Dad smiled a bit and simply said, 'Ok' as he left the room. "I know Dad was trying to protect me from being hurt."

"I understand that, Kate. He's simply a father who loves his daughter."

As we began to walk back to Kate's house it suddenly dawned on me. "Here it is July, Kate and …." A bit bewildered, she gave me a quizzical look. "What?" she asked.

"Think about it, Kate. We met in the summer of '65, where our love began and here it is summer again almost three years later and about to walk into the future together as husband and wife."

CHAPTER EIGHTEEN

WHERE IT BEGAN

*I*t was a clear, warm day at the park on the tenth day of July. The blue sky, gentle breeze and billowing clouds made the day even more beautiful. Sitting before the concession stand were family members and close friends. It was quite a sight, especially for the onlookers who were simply camping.

I was wearing a Navy-blue suit with a white shirt and light blue tie. My hair had not quite grown back to its normal length, but just enough for other people not to really notice. Tom was wearing blue sports jacket, white shirt and khaki slacks. I stood there in nervous anticipation. Kate and I decided not to have the traditional wedding music. Instead "Unchained Melody" by the Righteous Brothers would play quietly in the background.

"Oh, my love, my darling I've hungered for your touch...."

As the song began to play, Father O'Callaghan signaled for the guests to rise. From around the concession stand, I could see Kate arm in arm with her father, and Sharon, her Maid of Honor. Kate was wearing a beautiful white wedding dress and carrying a bouquet of red roses. I couldn't help noticing how her beautiful, soft blonde hair fell gently over her shoulders as her father took her hand and put it in mine.

"*...a long, lonely time....*"

As I stood at the front nervously holding Kate's hand and only half hearing Father O' Callaghan, I couldn't help but stare at this beautiful woman who had gone through so much. I didn't deserve such love and devotion. She could have any man yet, Kate loved me. How had I become so blessed? I have asked God that question over and over. One thing I knew for sure, I would love and honor Kate always.

"*Time goes by so slowly, and time can do so much.... are you still mine?*"

Gazing into Mike's eyes, I couldn't help but feel chills all over my body. Here we were standing before Father O'Callaghan about to commit our lives to one another. It had been a long, hard road since our first meeting here in what seems like ages ago. I have loved this man ever since we first skipped rocks across the river; ever since our first kiss. I had dreamed of Mike almost every night since that time. I almost lost him to a stupid war, but here we are, side by side. I'd stand beside him forever.

"*I need your love, I need your love, God speed your love to me....*"

After a reading from the First Letter of Paul to the Corinthians, Chapter 13, where it says, "Love is patient, love is kind...." and a brief talk about the beauty of marriage, Father O'Callaghan began:

"Do you, Michael Douglas Thompson, take Kathleen Anne Flynn to be your lawfully wedded wife pledging, before God and these witnesses to be unto her ever faithful, devoted and true?"

"I do."

"And will you sustain her in sickness and in health and in times of poverty, if they should come, as well as in prosperity?"

"I will."

"Do you, Kathleen Anne Flynn, take Michael Douglas Thompson to be your lawfully wedded husband, pledging before God and these witnesses to be unto him ever faithful, devoted and true?"

"I do."

"And will you sustain him in sickness and in health, in times of poverty, if they should come, as well as in prosperity?"

"I will."

Father O' Callaghan took the two rings. "These rings are a symbol reflecting the significance of the vows you offer each other here today. The circle is a design meant to be a constant reminder that your love for one another must never come to an end."

As Mike slipped the wedding ring onto my finger, I felt such joy as I had never felt before. Once again my heart was beating so fast I could hardly breathe.

"Lonely rivers flow to the sea...to the sea...to the open arms of the sea."

Staring into Mike's eyes, I placed the ring on his finger. We didn't have to speak. We knew what the other was thinking. We had come a long way since 1965, a summer in time.

"For as much as Mike and Kate have pledged their love and faith to one another and to God, and as they have sealed their love with the giving of rings and exchanging of vows, I pronounce that they are husband and wife."

"Lonely rivers sigh, wait for me, wait for me. I'll be coming home, wait for me.

Oh, my love, my darling, I've hungered, hungered for your touch a long, lonely time.

Time goes by so slowly. And time can do so much. Are you still mine?"

The End

Letters

July 10, 1967
An Khe, Vietnam (somewhere in the jungle)

My dearest Kate,

I don't have to look at my calendar to know what today is! How I wish I were there to wish you a happy birthday. Hopefully, this time next year we will celebrate it together.

I am sorry the letters have not been as frequent as before. We have been so busy going out on patrols that we hardly have time for anything else. As a matter of fact we are on a patrol now. I decided to skip the quick lunch break and scribble a few lines before we started off again. I'm sorry if the letter is dirty and a bit messy. I'm writing as fast as I can. I may not be able to finish now but I will eventually.

It has been very hot the last few days. And it seems to rain daily mostly in the morning so it gets muggy. The mosquitoes are almost unbearable. I'm glad when it rains because the mosquitoes are not as bothersome.

Dang, we just got word that we are moving out so I'll stop for now. Will write more in this letter the next stop we make.

I love you, Kate. Never forget that for one moment!!

Mike

July 12, 1967
An Khe

Well Kate, this is the first chance I have had to continue the letter
I began on your birthday. We are in our tents for the next couple
of days so I will have more time to finish this letter.

Again, it is raining and very muggy!!

I was thinking last night about our first meeting at the park.
How awkward I must have seemed to you. I remember almost
everything about that day. Talking on and on about what we liked
and finding out we had the same taste in music and television shows.
I remember us skipping rocks across the river. Mostly, I remember
the first kiss we had the second day. It was the very first real kiss
for me! Kate, I knew then and there that I loved you. I just knew it!

I am glad to be almost over my tour here. I am counting the
days. I have a calendar where I cross off each day as it goes by.
Most of us do that. Pretty soon I will be what we call a 'double digit
midget." That is someone with ninety-nine days or less in Vietnam.

Kate, I will be so glad when this tour is over because I have
been fortunate so far. The sad thing is I have lost three close friends
here. I am almost afraid to make friends now. I had a friend named
Pat who was hurt in our first fight with the Viet Cong. He had a
terrible stomach wound. We knew he would not live and I think he
knew it too. I cried when they took him away in a chopper. I cried
again when I saw his name listed as killed in action in the Army
Stars and Stripes newspaper. I don't know about this war anymore,
baby. I want to run from it, but I know I can't.

Well, it's quite dark now and hard to write. I will finish and
mail this tomorrow.

Love always,

Mike

July 18, 1967
An Khe

Hi, dear one,

I'm so sorry that I have not finished this letter and sent it. The day after I wrote the last part of the letter we were given a mission and were gone for five and a half days. I'm only now able to continue.

To be honest, Kitten, I am so very tired. We hiked through thick jungle brush the entire time we were out. We were all so dirty and sweaty and tempers flare. I can't say where we were or what we did but you can believe we put some hurt to the enemy. We had no one seriously hurt, thank God.

I have been thinking about our future. I know this is a lousy way to propose but I can't hold back any longer. Kate, would you marry me? I have loved you since our very first meeting. I don't have a heck of a lot to offer but I will work hard to be a good husband. My heart beats so fast every time I think of you. If you should say yes then I will plan on asking your parents when I get home. That may seem backwards but I just couldn't wait to ask you!

My thoughts of you every day are what keep me going here. I'm careful with every step I take when on patrol because I want to leave here in one piece and get back home to you.

I am going to end this letter so I can get it off on the mail. I'll be on pins and needles until I hear from you!!!

I love you with all my heart, Kate!!!

Mike

July 31, 1967

My dearest Mike,

Oh Mike, it was a beautiful proposal. YES!! I will marry you!! Being away from you has been the hardest thing I have had to endure in my life. I could never be more sure that you are the love of my life and I want to spend every minute with you forever. I want to be your wife and have a family together. I will support you always and respect you. When you return to Logan Airport, I will be there to fall into your arms and hope that there will never be such a distance between us again. You are and will always be my every heartbeat.

There was something so special about that day at Brandon State Park when I first met you. I felt an immediate connection. You were so happy and fun loving. I loved your red hair and blue eyes.

This connection stayed with me and I knew I couldn't wait to see you again and get to know you more.

It was hard to pack up and leave the park that weekend. I knew that I'd be waiting every day for the mailman to arrive in hopes that I would get a letter from you.

Just two days later, I was thrilled when I got your letter and your picture! I will keep it on my desk so you will always be in front of me and always in my thoughts and prayers. The letters and picture I will treasure forever.

Each day I wait for another letter and I always will write back to you right away.

Be safe my precious love and soldier.

Love always, Kate

August 10, 1967
An Khe, Vietnam

Dearest Kate:

YIPPEE!!! I just got your letter saying you will marry me!! Oh, Kate, I am so happy. I'll be the best husband I can be!! I can't wait to speak with your parents. It is hard to believe that my tour is almost over. In a few weeks we will be together again soon and begin pick up our lives where we left off. I've been so lucky to come through this year unscathed.

The joy in leaving here is lessened by the fact that I lost friends. I feel a bit guilty at times because I will get home to you while some my friends will never get to see their loved ones. All because of a stupid war that we are most likely not going to win in the end. So much blood and carnage, Kate. So sad.

We have been in base camp for a week now. That is unusual for us. I have been gathering my things and sending home knick-knacks that I have bought here and there. On the last day, I will board a civilian plane and fly to California. We are scheduled to land at Oakland and then I will take a plane to Logan from there.

Sorry, Kate, but I need to make this letter short! Another mission! I'll send another soon!

I love you, Kate, and am the happiest guy in the world!!!!

Mike

November 23, 1967
An Khe, Vietnam

My soon to be Bride,

Just finished another mission. Man, am I ever tired. We walked through jungle brush, rice paddies, and on muddy roads for three days. So much rain and mud. I often wonder how much we actually accomplish.

I just took my first warm shower since before we left. Man, that water felt so good. I had to scrub and scrape the mud and crud off of my body. We all did. Just picture seven guys in a shower room all scrubbing our skin raw. But we are laughing and cutting up. Three of us are leaving in the next couple of days.

When I come home I hope you will not be too shocked at how I look. I have gained weight and gained a few wrinkles here and there. My skin is quite dry from the constant beating of the sun.

I will call you from California when I get in and let you know flight details.

I just had a talk with my commander and he asked me if I would fly one last mission. I really didn't want to go, being so close to my leaving in a couple of days, but it has to do with some of my fellow soldiers. I can't go into details but I want to help my brothers. They would do the same for me.

When I get back from our mission I will pick up my orders and head to the transfer point for a flight home.

I have to go for now. I need to grab some gear and get to the chopper.

Remember, Kate. I love you with all of my heart.

Mike